Death at Abbey Road

Rachel McLean writes thrillers that make your pulse race and your brain tick. Originally a self-publishing sensation, she has sold millions of copies digitally, with massive success in the UK, and a growing reach internationally. She is the author of the Dorset Crime novels and the spin-off McBride & Tanner series and Cumbria Crime series. In 2021, she won the Kindle Storyteller Award with *The Corfe Castle Murders* and her books regularly hit No1 in the Bookstat ebook chart on launch.

Millie Ravensworth is the pen name of two authors who have been writing entertaining novels together for more than ten years. The Millie Ravensworth books focus on their shared love of crime stories and charming characters who readers love spending time with.

Also by Rachel McLean and Millie Ravensworth

The London Cosy Mysteries series

Death at Westminster
Death in the West End
Death at Tower Bridge
Death on the Thames
Death at St Paul's Cathedral
Death at Abbey Road

RACHEL McLEAN
MiLLiE RAVENSWORTH

LONDON COSY MYSTERIES BOOK 6

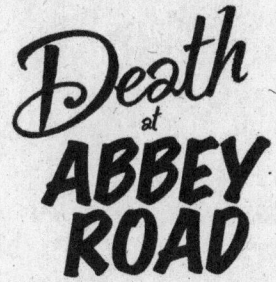

Death at ABBEY ROAD

ACKROYD PUBLISHING

Ackroyd Publishing

ackroydpublishing.com

Printed and bound in the UK by CPI Group (Uk) Ltd, Croydon CR0 4YY

Chapter One

Diana Bakewell strolled along Abbey Road, her colleague Zaf Williams at her side.

"Wave to the webcam!" said Zaf.

Diana gave a small smile. There was a camera trained on the zebra crossing not far from the Abbey Road Studios, so people could find images of themselves crossing the road in the style of the famous Beatles album cover.

"You'd think it would cut down on road rage incidents," added Zaf, wincing as a van leaned on its horn. A group of tourists were taking it in turns to walk halfway across the road to pose for each other's pictures. There were at least twenty of them, blocking traffic, and the drivers were becoming frustrated.

"People come from all over the world to see this crossing," said Diana. "Getting the picture they want is important to them."

Zaf nodded. "I wonder if there's a way of timing our tour so that we can come here when the traffic is lightest?"

"A good point."

She and Zaf were refining the details for a Beatles walking tour for Chartwell and Crouch. Until recently, the company had been mostly focused on bus tours for the many domestic and international tourists visiting London but now, the business was in such financial trouble that their vintage Routemaster buses were being sold off one by one. Privately, Diana wasn't sure even these desperate measures would be enough to stave off the company's inevitable collapse.

Diana, in her mid-sixties now, had been with Chartwell and Crouch for many years. She had seen the Marylebone depot go from the strong and stable management style of Morris Walker to the narrow-minded and penny-pinching regime of Paul Kensington. The tighter the grip he tried to keep on Chartwell and Crouch's finances, the faster the money seemed to slip through his fingers. And even young Zaf, a bright and energetic outsider from Birmingham who had been with the company for less than two years, seemed to have been hit hard by the possibility of their company and jobs disappearing for good.

"People will want to go in the Abbey Road shop," said Diana, pointing to the building just beyond the studios. "There's no point getting here at the crack of dawn."

Zaf smiled. "A Beatles experience probably involves buying some memorabilia."

She looked at him, then glanced at the young tourists by the zebra crossing. "I'm surprised the Beatles still seem relevant to so many young people."

"Bit more your era," said Zaf.

"Hardly. I wasn't even at primary school when they hit the charts. They'd split up before I reached secondary school. Doesn't mean I didn't know all about them, though."

"Yeah, yeah," said Zaf, waving away a familiar story. "You rented your flat off George Harrison. I know."

"My former flat. Now, my mum – who I'm obviously delighted to be sharing a flat with – she would have been a bit old for Beatlemania, but we did have their music in our house. *Magical Mystery Tour, Let it Be...* Well, I never."

"Well, I never? Don't know that one."

She pointed across the road at a large square house on a corner plot off Abbey Road. This part of leafy St John's Wood was full of large houses, from Georgian mansions to twentieth-century Art Deco apartment blocks. High walls and big square buildings were very much the style. It had taken Diana a moment to recognise this particular one.

"I know that building," she said. "Know it very well. Used to be Grove End Studios."

"Another recording studio?"

"The old owner insisted he hadn't set it up here to catch a bit of the Abbey Road magic, but who knows? If that was the idea, it didn't work. The place has been derelict for years."

"Well, that front bit's a café," Zaf pointed out.

The front left wing of the building had been converted into a café with a bold red, white and black frontage.

"Let it Bean," he said, reading the café name. "Oh, I get it. That's good. And it's probably time for a cuppa, yeah?"

They crossed back over the Abbey Road zebra crossing, avoiding posing tourists and peeved London drivers.

"You know, people shouldn't tempt fate," said Diana. "That Abbey Road album cover was thought by some to be a coded message about Paul McCartney's death."

"But Paul McCartney isn't dead," said Zaf, frowning.

"You clearly don't know the crazy theories, Zaf. Paul's dead, baby. Paul's dead."

Chapter Two

The *Let it Bean* café had taken the Beatles theme and squeezed everything it could from it. The windows were full of memorabilia, including fake Abbey Road street signs, Beatles action figures and mugs printed with Beatles lyrics. The walls featured album covers and the menu was filled with tortured puns. It was an absorbing read, handwritten neatly on a chalkboard above the counter.

"I can't decide between the *I want to Hold your Ham and cheese croissant* and the *I am the Walnut cookie*," said Zaf.

Diana looked down to order some tea and recognised the man behind the counter. "Oh goodness me, Chaz!"

Zaf followed her gaze and pulled on a polite smile. He'd met Chaz Chase on a number of occasions. Each time the man seemed to be fulfilling a different role – taxi driver, pub landlord, et cetera – but whatever the occasion, Zaf was always reminded that this shaven-headed character was the hard-as-steel right hand man to Big Ernie Holland. Both Chaz and Ernie gave off a cheery East End businessman vibe but Zaf knew that business was a dodgy as a seven pound note. They weren't men to get on the wrong side of, even if Big Ernie treated Diana like a much-loved niece.

"Awright, Diana," said Chaz, grinning. It was a nice enough smile, but there was a predatory edge to it. He winked at Zaf. "Bet you're wondering why I'm here in me pinny, eh?"

"Hadn't even crossed my mind," said Zaf.

"I've been branching out. Restaurant business. This place hasn't been open long, but I'm getting reviews and good custom."

Diana gestured towards the neat tables and the fresh decor. "I can see this becoming a magnet for tourists. I love the menu!"

"Dream of mine. Most of the memorabilia's from me own collection," said Chaz. "Love The Beatles."

"Really?" said Zaf.

Chaz eyed him. "Yeah, they might have been a bunch of Northern monkeys, but they made London their own. Siddown. I'll bring yer stuff over."

They found a table in the window. Zaf looked over the notes they'd made for their walking tour. *Abbey Road, the Cavendish Avenue house Paul McCartney bought in sixty-five, a wander down to Marylebone Station where A Hard Day's Night was filmed...* It was shaping up into a decent tour.

Chaz bustled over with a tray and placed it on the table between them.

"Here we go. Pot of tea for two, your croissant, Zaf, and a complimentary *Long and Winding Rocky Road* for each of you. Freshly made."

Their tea mugs had Beatles lyrics printed on them. Diana's said *All You Need is Love.* Zaf's had *I Get By with a Little Help from my Friends* printed on it in jolly letters.

"Thanks, Chaz," said Diana. "It's a surprise to be back in this building, even a part of it."

"Of course," said Chaz.

"You recorded here?" said Zaf, realising he was slow on the uptake.

In the eighties, Diana had been part of a pop group, ElectraBeat. They'd had that one stonking hit, *Count Me In*, in eighty-one, one hit album and a number of so-so albums before an acrimonious split at the end of the decade.

"I did," she replied. "Grove End Studios is where the so-called magic happened."

Chaz slapped his sizeable forehead. "I didn't tell ya, did I?"

"Tell us what?"

"I don't just own the caff. I own the whole place."

The whole building? Zaf wondered how much this huge old house would be worth and how deep Chaz's dodgy pockets were.

"This ruin?" asked Diana with a concerned smile.

"I've had it refurbed," said Chaz. "All done, really. Even got your old bandmates Pascal and Ken to check it from a technical perspective. Started me own record label. Lamé Records. You know, sparkly and shiny. Can't believe I didn't tell you, of all people! I'm having a launch party next Friday."

"Oh!"

"I was going to get in touch with you, see if you'd attend as one of our VIP guests." He turned to Zaf. "You're invited an' all, Zaf. Bring that crowd from work. The more the merrier."

"And, um," said Diana, "I suppose you've already invited the other band members."

Chaz couldn't hold back a smile. "Ariadne. Yeah, I know she an' you have got beef. I don't know if she an' Pascal are even talking to each other. But she'll be there."

Zaf could see Diana trying to avoid his eye. Diana and Ariadne did not get on. They'd grown up in the East End together. As teenagers they'd shared a flat, and they'd joined ElectraBeat together. They'd even both gone into the tour guide business, albeit for different companies. So alike, but they could rarely stand each other in anything but the smallest of doses.

"We'll have all of ElectraBeat there," said Chaz. "Well, obviously not Morris."

"Obviously." Diana gave a sad smile. "Being in prison plays havoc with a person's social life."

"Tell me about it," said Chaz with heavy emphasis. "Well, anyway, we want to honour the past. We're keen to keep it authentic. You never know, there might come a time when people want to go on tours of this studio, once we've made it famous again, eh?"

He looked at the album sleeve for Abbey Road on the wall above their heads, as though imagining what hit records his newly-acquired studio might produce.

"Diana was telling me that this cover is a coded message about Paul McCartney's death," said Zaf.

"Of course," said Chaz. He pointed at the Fab Four on the zebra crossing. "This is a funeral procession. John in white is a holy figure, Ringo in a suit is the undertaker and George in his denims there is the gravedigger. Paul's out of step with the rest and he's barefoot. He's the corpse."

"But, just to be clear, Paul isn't dead," said Zaf.

Chaz gave him a look. "For those who are prepared to see the signs, Paul's death is an absolute fact."

Zaf thought that was crazy enough to make a note of in his pad.

Chapter Three

When they returned to Chartwell and Crouch's depot in Marylebone, bus driver Newton Crombie was polishing the interior of the last remaining tour bus. Diana was certain he'd polished it the day before, but Newton was mourning its loss already; soon enough it would be gone to a new owner.

Gus, the depot cat, sat on the bus's bright red bonnet and watched his adopted human go about his sad cleaning rituals.

Diana went to find Paul Kensington.

She sighed and knocked on the door of his office just as her phone buzzed. It was Pascal Palmer. She was halfway in before she realised she had already answered it.

"Oh, hello, Pascal," she said.

The depot manager looked up from the box of files and office junk he was rooting through. She put up a finger to him – *one minute.*

"Ah, Diana," said her old friend. "How are you?"

"Sorry, I accidentally answered while I'm at work. Can I call you back?"

Paul Kensington was frowning. In his hand he had a key on a plastic fob, and he was turning it over as if trying to work out what it was for.

"Oh, my dear," said Pascal in his rich deep voice, "I just wanted to check if you were going to this do at Mr Chase's new music studio."

"I was planning to."

"Because I thought you should know he also reached out to Ariadne and me."

She could read him entirely. "You're worried that if the three of us are in the same room together, there will be fireworks?"

"More like nuclear explosions."

She shrugged. "I'm going. I'd love to see the old place. Guess we'll have to turn up wearing our toughest armour."

Paul's frown had deepened. He held up the key. "Do you know why we have a key for Baker Street Luggage Drop?"

"You have company," said Pascal, seeming to sense the awkwardness. "A colleague?"

"My manager. We'll speak later."

"Of course, my dear."

Diana hung up and looked at Paul. "Paul – sorry – could I please have a word?"

Paul was still holding out the key, his eyes furiously questioning.

"No idea," she said.

He tossed the key back into the box and flipped through some papers. "It will have to be a quick word. You can see I'm busy."

Diana had no idea how he could be truly busy. Bookings were thin on the ground and there was increasingly little for them to do.

Diana sat down on the chair in front of his desk. "Paul, I sent you a business plan yesterday."

"Yes?"

"I think it could work to get us back on track."

"Back on track?"

She waved her hand at the depot beyond his office. In a company that seemed to be falling apart, this tiny office felt more and more like the emergency bunker of a dictator in his final days.

"Did you get a chance to take a look?" she asked.

Paul gave a tiny laugh and shook his head. "Goodness me, Diana, I can't fault your enthusiasm, can I? Is there anything you won't have a go at?"

Diana forced her face to stay neutral. "I'm sorry, Paul, but did you look at it or not?"

Paul adjusted his tie. He always wore a neatly tied tie with the short sleeved shirts he favoured. "I'm afraid that I didn't. I'm not sure you realise how busy I am right now, Diana. It's nice of you to try and help, but you should probably stick to the things you know about, eh?"

"Has the fact that Chartwell and Crouch sponsored my part time degree in business economics slipped your mind?" asked Diana.

"Is that right?" he said, either indifferent or oblivious. "Well, that must have been before my time. I'll try and take a look. Leave it with me."

Diana had been dismissed. She stood to leave his office.

"I'm sure you don't have time because you're so busy, but we've all been invited to a launch event at the new Grove End Studios in St John's Wood next Friday. Just mentioning it, but I doubt—"

"Oh, that sounds fun," he said. "Yes, I think I already had

an invite somewhere. It would be good. Chance for a bit of social team-building."

Team-building? The very notion seemed ridiculous after the man's inertia and ineptitude had all but obliterated the team. Diana left the office and closed the door behind her with a small grunt of frustration.

Paul Kensington was incompetent and unrepentant. The sooner he was gone from Chartwell and Crouch, the better.

Chapter Four

Zaf walked through the quiet, tidy streets of St John's Wood, curious about how the launch event would play out. Diana had focused on work all week, and hadn't made much of the upcoming event. She was sometimes reluctant to talk about her brief spell as a chart-topping act. If Zaf had been a famous musician, he was sure he'd dine out on it for the rest of his life.

Maybe, he thought, as he paused to cross Abbey Road, this event would fill in some of the blanks in what he knew of Diana's history.

Zaf had already decided that if ever an occasion demanded a vintage velvet suit in lime green, then it was this one. Months before, he'd been allowed to choose some outfits from the wardrobe of Bryan, Diana's recently deceased upstairs neighbour. Bryan had possibly been part of the same music scene as the Beatles, and had left behind some amazing clothes. It felt right to bring Bryan's suit along for the ride.

The entrance to Grove End Studios was an understated

door to the side of the *Let it Bean* café. Zaf paused, then shook his head. Why wouldn't it be? This was a working building.

There was a woman in a high-collared white shirt with a clipboard in the reception area.

"Name?"

She didn't look like a receptionist, mainly because she hadn't got the memo about smiling as she greeted newcomers.

"Zaf Williams."

She made a mark on her clipboard. "Down the corridor and to the left."

Zaf followed the instructions. The reception area had looked like the boring front offices of any saw business, but as he walked down the stark white corridor running the length of the building, he got a sudden feel for the uniqueness of this place. It might have been an old house but it was a deep, deep building. The corridor was long enough for at least twenty framed photos of bands that had recorded here before he reached the aforementioned door.

A waitress with a platter of champagne glasses nodded for him to take one and go inside.

At first glance, the room beyond was much like the hall at Zaf's old primary school: large, high-ceilinged with windows only at the very top. But no school hall had microphone stands across the floor, nor an upper gallery with a large control room overlooking the hall.

"This is cool," he murmured.

Eighties synth music played softly from hidden speakers, filling the cavernous space in a way the visiting guests could not.

Chaz appeared and clapped Zaf on the shoulder. "Zaf. Glad ya could make it to the Lamé Records launch." He eyed

Zaf's suit. "Either you know more about fashion than I do, or you lost a bet."

"My boyfriend said something similar."

Chaz looked past Zaf. "Brought 'im with you?"

"He had other commitments. His dad flew in for dinner."

Chaz jutted his chin. "Well, the gang's all here," he said, gesturing at the two dozen guests milling about the place. "You met my sound engineer out front?"

"Sound engineer?"

"Tracy Chen, out in reception. Think she's decided to be bouncer for the evening. I don't care who turns up." He looked over at an approaching figure. "Well, some I'd rather avoid..." He gave Zaf a curt nod and went off to greet other people.

Zaf recognised the approaching figure by his white linen suit before he recognised his face. Diana had mentioned that Pascal Palmer liked to dress like 'the man from Del Monte', but only now did Zaf realise what that meant.

Pascal Palmer, tall, regal and looking good for a man nearing seventy, had been part of the ElectraBeat group with Diana, but for the last two decades, he had been working as a restaurant critic. Zaf had met him at Diana's last birthday party and they'd got on well, despite some confusion over Pascal's relationship with Diana.

Pascal held out a small pastry confection from the buffet.

"What would you call this?" he asked.

"A vol-au-vent."

"More like a pastry bullet." Pascal placed it on an empty table, uneaten. "How are you doing, young sir? Love the suit."

"Thank you. This space is amazing."

Pascal raised his eyes to the ceiling. "I'd forgotten how big this place was. Studio two upstairs isn't much smaller, and then studio three on the top floor is a bit more intimate. Possibly my favourite."

"I don't think I've ever been to a proper recording studio."

"Magical places. You can make anything happen here." He turned so that he and Zaf were facing the same way, looking at the mingling guests. "I don't know if I'm being chivalrous and making sure my ex doesn't have to meet me, or just acting like a coward."

Across the way was Ariadne Webb, talking and laughing with a circle of people. She and Pascal had been a couple, but that had ended badly many years earlier.

"That's Tom Griffin with her, you know him?" said Pascal.

"Boss of ACE Tours," said Zaf. "Nice guy, everyone says."

"I thought he was the rival to your company. Driving you lot out of business."

"Oh, we don't need anyone else to help us do that," said Zaf. "Diana and Ariadne snipe at each other but ACE Tours seems a decent company to work for."

"Ha! If that's what you think, perhaps you ought to go over and ingratiate yourself. Get yourself a new job before the bad ship Chartwell and Crouch sinks for good." Pascal raised his glass of orange juice and pointed across the way. "I'm going to talk to Ken, our old keyboardist. He went on the hippie trail after the band split and I hear he has some insane notions for his next musical project."

"Oh?"

Pascal smiled. "If the rumours are to be believed, a concept album so insane it might bankrupt this studio before it's even got started. Enjoy your evening, Zaf. Nothing lasts."

With that, he crossed the studio floor and disappeared into the crowd.

Chapter Five

Diana couldn't miss Zaf's arrival, not with him wearing such a bright suit. She waved, but he didn't seem to see her.

She was standing next to Big Ernie Holland. Big Ernie was a good few years older than her but life didn't seem to want to slow this man down. Ernie was very much an uncle figure in Diana's life. But for all his generosity, she knew he had a darker side.

"So, how's livin' with your old mum?" Ernie asked.

"It's not so bad."

Ernie laughed. "I love Beverley Bakewell but if I had to live with that tough old bird one of us would be dead within a week."

Diana nodded. "I miss my flat. But we've settled into a sort of truce."

"Well, your stuff's safe in storage 'til you get back on your feet," said Ernie. "It can sit there for years if it needs to."

Diana smiled. Ernie had helped her with the move, when she was forced out of her grand Pimlico flat in Eccleston

Square. He owned the storage facility where nearly all of her possessions now resided. She had a sneaking suspicion that they would stay there until she either died or decided to get rid of them all. There was no 'getting back on her feet', not on a tour guide's salary. It wasn't a topic worth contemplating.

"What do you think of Chaz's new venture then?" she asked. "He looks as if he's enjoying the role of host this evening."

"He's got hidden depths, has Chaz," said Ernie proudly. "Got a lot of investors in his Lame Records."

"I think it's pronounced *lamé*, Ernie. I wondered if Chaz might have struggled to get respectable investors with his background."

"Who says his investors are respectable?" Ernie grinned. "He's proper made up that you could come tonight. You and Ariadne being here years ago has given him that connection to the past that he loves. I think he said he'd found some old pictures."

"Oh really?" Diana wondered what pictures they might be. It was a while since she'd had any reason to think about her time here. "It's funny being back here. It hasn't changed a bit."

She looked at her former bandmates. Ariadne and Pascal were keeping a wary distance from one another, avoiding each other's orbits. Beyond them, Zaf was talking to ElectraBeat's old keyboard player, Ken Ferrari. Between Zaf's green suit and Ken's bright pink shirt, it was hard to know which of them was the most colourful. She hadn't spoken to Ken in maybe five years. He'd always been so self-contained, a man fizzing with creative ideas, although not all of them good. Ariadne, Pascal, Ken...

"Shame Morris can't be here too," said Ernie.

"It is."

"How long has he got to serve still?"

The sentence for Morris Walker's embezzlement conviction had been all the longer for his refusal to return any of the money he had supposedly stolen.

"Too long," she replied. "He's not a young man now."

Ernie stretched his back, pushing his elbows out. "None of us are. You still cling to this idea he was innocent."

"I do."

Ernie gave her a wry smile. "Find me a single bloke inside who won't swear on his mother's grave that he's innocent."

"I'm serious, Ernie. And one day it'll come to light, you mark my words. There's just too many holes in that story. He was supposed to have set up those fake websites selling fake tickets. They were all in his name, for crying out loud! Morris was never that daft."

Ernie nodded. "He didn't seem like an idiot, I'll give you that. But his alibi for the day he withdrew the cash from that bank..."

"I'm investigating that. I'm chasing down a Pomeranian dog called Marengo."

"You are?" Ernie raised an eyebrow. "Well, good luck to you. I say that if a criminal wants money to stay hidden, it's not too hard for them to do it, if they know what they're doing. Hiding money is a dark art." He grinned again, looking across the room at Chaz.

"Do I really want to know?" said Diana.

Ernie wrinkled his nose. "No, darlin'. I like you sweet and innocent."

Chapter Six

Zaf found Ken Ferrari fascinating. Fascinating, and possibly mentally unhinged. Ken was a stooped man in his late sixties, round-lensed specs and wispy beard lending him a mystical aura. Zaf wondered if he'd done a lot of drugs during his musical heyday. That would at least explain the weird avenue their conversation had gone down.

"A cat album?" he asked.

"A cat album," said Ken.

"Not a recording of Cats the musical?"

"No. A cat album."

Ken had drawn in an audience including Newton Crombie, Paul Kensington, Pascal Palmer and Tom Griffin from ACE Tours.

"Newton here tells me you have a cat down at your depot," said Ken.

"He's not an official cat," replied Paul Kensington. "An unwanted tenant."

"People love cats," said Ken. "People spoil their cats rotten. I love my Captain Smudginson."

"Captain Smudginson?" repeated Tom Griffin with a smile.

"I love him," said Ken. "You can get them videos where it's like an hour of birds on a ledge, or you can have them play a game where they pat the wiggly goldfish on an iPad to score points."

"Newton's done all that for Gus," said Zaf.

"Right! Well here's the thing. I'm not sure anyone's ever made a whole album of songs for cats. For cats and by cats, cos some of them are quite vocal an' all, aren't they? I reckon it would be a runaway success."

His grinning face told Zaf he was convinced he'd hit on a winning formula, but Zaf wasn't so sure.

"So is it for cats or by cats?" asked Tom. "They sound like two different things."

"Nah, it's definitely both. It's a concept album, see?"

"Concept album. Right."

"No, no," said Paul, imperiously. "Recording albums is so passé. You should be renting this space out to people who record podcasts."

"Oh, in the business, are you, mate?" asked Ken.

"A related field," replied Paul.

"Tourist tours a related field...?" asked Tom.

Paul gave him a look. "It's all entertainment."

Ken was ignoring him. "So I reckon you should bring your cat along, Newton."

"Bring Gus?" said Newton, clearly intrigued.

Ken nodded vigorously. "We can get some samples off him. Make it worth his while with catnip."

"I think you should get involved, Newton," said Zaf. It might distract Newton from the loss of his buses.

Newton frowned.

"You should set up some sessions with Gus, absolutely," Zaf continued. "He could be a recording star."

"No, no, I think you've got it wrong," said Paul. "Podcasts. Voiceovers. Music recording is dead."

Ken gave a sharp laugh. "Music never dies, mate. It's what makes us human. And recording music... that's capturing dreams, freezing them in a moment. The stories this building could tell. The other week, I pointed Pascal towards some old demo tapes of ours I found in Studio Three. One listen to them and the man was transported. Transported."

"No, hear me out," Paul continued, oblivious to the man's passion. "I've got some ideas I want to put your way. If you'll excuse us." He put his arm around Ken's shoulder and steered him away. "Now, I'm working on this great little enterprise called the Londiniumarium, and I've recently got some high level funding for..."

Zaf, Newton and Tom Griffin watched him go.

"Your boss..." began Tom.

"He's a complete twonk," said Newton.

Tom frowned. "I try not to speak ill of the competition."

"Oh, please do," said Zaf. "He's a constant thorn in our sides."

"The sooner he dies, the better," added Newton.

Zaf was about to contradict his colleague, but at that moment, his phone rang: his boyfriend, Alexsei.

"Excuse me," he said to Tom and Newton. "I need to take this."

He stepped away and put the phone to his ear. "Hello?"

There was swirling static on the line, punctuated with fractions of speech.

"Alexsei," Zaf said. "I can't hear you."

He moved to the centre of the room. The swirling was still there. He stepped out into the corridor.

"Hello?"

"Bad signal." The unfriendly woman from the front door was calling to him down the corridor. Tracy Chen.

"Sorry?" said Zaf.

"It's a very bad signal in this area," she explained. "Go upstairs and out on the fire escape."

"What?"

"The fire escape. It's safe. Or go on the roof. Maybe less safe."

Zaf hesitated. Tracy gave an exasperated sigh and came marching down the corridor. She gestured for him to follow her up to the first floor, where she pointed at a door that led through to an external metal staircase.

The call to Alexsei had dropped but Zaf went out onto the fire escape anyway. It was one of those zig-zagging metal staircases.

The steps clanged under his feet as he climbed, and he wondered why it always felt precarious on stairs where you could see through the gaps. He tried to call Alexsei again.

"Hello?"

"Ah! Finally I can hear you," said Alexsei. "Where are you?"

Zaf was almost at the top. "I'm on the roof of Grove End Studios looking out over Abbey Road from up high."

"Yeah? Can you see anything interesting?"

"Mostly I can see the tops of trees and the chimneys of houses."

"Didn't the Beatles do a concert on the top of the Abbey Road studio?" asked Alexsei.

"No, that was at Savile Row, on top of the Apple building. That's Apple the record company, not the other one."

"One of the things I like about you, you know a lot of fun facts," said Alexsei.

"Diana and I have been working on a Beatles walking tour."

Alexsei sighed. He'd suggested to Zaf that if his days at Chartwell and Crouch were numbered, he should divert his energy into finding an alternative.

"I should get back to the party," said Zaf. "Aren't you having dinner with your dad?"

"We finished early. We came to an arrangement."

"Oh?"

Another sigh. Alexsei's father, Kamran Dadashov, owned significant engineering and property interests in every country between here and his native Azerbaijan. Most of the time it was a long distance relationship, and it hadn't been an easy one of late.

"He asked me to apologise," said Alexsei.

"For what?"

"For everything. For you."

"For me?"

"For taking your side in the business over the Eccleston Square house. For, in his words, 'flouncing off like a rebellious teen.' He did not mince his words."

"I thought you said you'd reached an agreement."

"It was possibly one-sided," said Alexsei. Zaf could hear sadness in his voice. "I told him he didn't need to come to London to see me ever again until he was ready to apologise and treat me like the adult I am."

"Oh, man," said Zaf. "He's your dad. Don't do this for me."

"I'm not doing it for you," Alexsei replied. "Well, I'm doing it for us. That's it. Ties cut. I'll just have to cope as a penniless dilettante socialite in London."

"With a luxury Thames apartment and a squillion in savings."

"It's a tough life." Alexsei gave a pretend tearful sniff.

Zaf smiled. "I love you."

"Good," said Alexsei. "I'm kind of banking on that."

"But he is your dad. Don't... don't let something like this hang over you. He won't be around forever and we can't rebuild relationships once someone has gone."

"I know," said Alexsei. "Anyway, I wondered if there was any point in me coming down to your party?"

"Absolutely. There's actual B-list popstars here. Super kitsch."

"I'll jump in a cab."

The call over, Zaf looked across the city. A sky of red and pink was settling across west London. He drank it in for a moment, then went back down the fire exit. There were fire doors leading off from the second and first floor but only the first floor one was open.

He returned to the warmth of the studio building. The night air was turning chilly.

Chapter Seven

Diana hadn't hesitated when Chaz suggested that people explore the recording spaces. Ken Ferrari led the way up to Studio Two on the first floor. Diana found herself walking beside Tom Griffin.

"This is all very exciting," he said.

"We had a lot of fun here," Diana told him.

"Ha!" added Ariadne, following them up the stairs. "And a lot of blazing rows."

Diana gave her a reproachful look.

"But it was also magical," agreed Ariadne, pausing to take a sip of champagne.

Studio Two was a large space with two booths and a control room in the far corner.

Tom and Diana followed Ken into the control booth. It had been a long time since she'd been in a studio. She peered at the knobs and dials on the old-school sound engineer's deck.

"Care to show me the ropes?" said Tom.

"If we touch any of these controls, I'm afraid Tracy Chen

could well hunt us down and kill us," replied Ken in a theatrical stage whisper.

"I thought you were her boss," said Diana.

"You know I don't do conflict."

Tom turned away from the controls and pulled open a cupboard door. "Have you noticed how much storage there is in this place?"

"I think we've even got some old instruments in there," said Ken. "Studio One is fully revamped but the higher you get, the more ancient the artifacts. It's like archaeology in reverse."

Tom leaned into the cupboard and answered with the *tss, tss, tss* of a cymbal being tapped with a fingernail.

"I wonder who it belongs to?" said Diana.

She saw the glow of his phone as he used it as a torch. "There's a label on the floor that says *Duran Duran*."

"Wow," said Diana. "Duran Duran's cymbal. A piece of pop history."

"Valuable to the right buyer," added Paul, crowding in behind them.

"Oh, this place is a treasure trove," said Tom.

"Of memories," agreed Diana. "This studio is where we recorded our second album, *Taunt*. Both Morris and Pascal used to spend a lot of time in here with the engineers."

"Hang on," said Tom. "But they were in the band, weren't they? How did they...?"

"Morris was the singer," said Ariadne in the doorway. "He used to get most of the other parts down and record his vocals separately."

"Didn't he say it helped him with his phrasing?" Diana asked Ariadne.

"God, yes! Yes, he did. So, he could be doing his thing here while we listened to his vocals in the booth."

"And Pascal was on drums. He spent a lot of time in the live room, but the two of them used to have these hand signals that they'd use through the glass." Diana felt like she was watching the echoes of their former selves, as they were back in the eighties. "Where is Pascal anyway?"

"Searching for old demo tapes in Studio Three upstairs I think," said Zaf, appearing at the door.

"Scrabbling around for souvenirs and past glories," tutted Paul. "Oh, if you'd had me as your manager back in those days, Diana ..."

"I dread to think," she said.

"The music industry is terribly fickle," said Ken. "You see the thing about it in those days was—"

"Sorry, Ken," said Paul, holding up a silencing hand and a buzzing phone. "I need to take this."

Diana gave Ken an apologetic shrug as Paul went outside into the main part of the studio. "Hello? Hello?"

"You guys deserve medals for working with him, don't you?" said Tom.

Through the control room window, they could see Paul wandering around the space, trying to find a signal.

"Diana here would make an infinitely better manager than Paul," said Zaf.

"Not something we'll ever be able to put to the test," replied Diana.

"You know, if you have any vacancies going, Tom," said Zaf with exaggerated eyebrow waggles, "you could do worse than our Diana."

"Don't put ideas into Tom's head," said Ariadne. She looked at her champagne glass. "I need a refill."

Zaf went out into the studio to talk to Paul. Diana watched him gesturing out and up, giving directions.

"Your friend speaks highly of you," Tom said to Diana.

"I'm happy where I am," she replied.

"Happy?" said Tom.

"Maybe not happy. But I don't quit when things get tough."

"We all quit ElectraBeat in the end," said Ken.

"That was different," said Diana. "We were all at each other's throats in the end. Ariadne and Pascal can barely stand each other even now."

Chapter Eight

Zaf pointed Paul Kensington to the fire exit on the first floor.

"The roof?" said Paul.

"The roof. It's perfectly safe."

Zaf was tempted to let the fire door close fully behind the manager, but his innate goodness got the better of him.

He turned as Diana, Ken Ferrari and Tom Griffin emerged from Studio Two.

"Told Paul to go to the roof to get a signal," said Zaf.

"Quite right," said Ken.

"Maybe we should return to the party downstairs," said Diana. "We're officially here to celebrate Chaz's venture after all."

"We can explore in a bit." Tom flinched at a sudden sound from upstairs. A slam, followed by shout of rage.

Even from a floor below, Zaf could hear a voice shout, "What the hell do you want?", followed by another slamming sound.

"What's that?" said Tom.

"Is that Pascal?" said Diana.

There was another shout. Pascal Palmer? A shout of pain?

Tom Griffin dashed for the stairs and Zaf chased after him. It was a long flight of stairs up to the second floor. The sparkle of the lower two floors was less evident here. There was peeling paint and grime on the floor of the long corridor. All the doors were closed.

"Where is he?" said Zaf.

He was answered by raised voices from a door to the rear of the building marked Studio Three.

"Give it to me!" demanded a voice.

"Who are you? Why are you—?" There was a clatter and groan of pain from Pascal.

Tom went to open the door. It didn't budge.

He hammered his fist on it. "Open up!"

"Pascal!" Zaf shouted, as if that might achieve something.

The voices from within had been replaced by the sounds of what seemed to be a violent struggle.

"What's happening?" asked Ken as he and Diana made it to the top of the stairs.

Zaf turned to Ken, hands outstretched. "Keys!"

Ken pushed his little round specs up his nose. "The master set are... I gave the keys to Pascal."

"Break it in," urged Diana.

Zaf gave her a look. He was capable of many things but, physically, he was built for speed and grace and looking damned fine in a suit. Brute strength was not him.

The struggles seemed to have stopped. As Zaf cocked an ear, there came a fresh sound. Smashing glass.

"A window?" said Ken.

A recollection of the outside rear of the building struck Zaf. "The fire escape!"

He looked around and tried to orientate himself, to match this second floor interior to what he'd seen on the fire escape.

"The fire exit on this floor?" he asked Ken. The old man pointed at the locked door.

Zaf grunted. "Flipping health and safety hazard!" He ran for the stairs heading back down. "Someone call the police!"

He flew downstairs, jumping the last five, turned back towards the fire exit door he'd let Paul through, and ran out. He looked up. There was no one on the fire escape. There was a scream of alarm below him.

He looked over the side into the grey alleyway that ran along the back of the studio building. Below and to the side, a rear door had opened and people were spilling out of it – Newton, Ariadne, Big Ernie Holland. But directly below Zaf, sprawled on the uneven tarmac of the alley, was a body.

The dead man lay on his back, arms outstretched like Jesus on the cross. One leg was bent under the other and – it would later occur to Zaf how odd it was that such tiny details stuck in the brain – there was one shoe missing and a pale sock on show. But it took him a second or two to note the most obvious thing.

The body on the ground wasn't Pascal Palmer.

Chapter Nine

D iana's attention was focused on the studio door in front of them. Ken had charged and bounced off it, yelling and clutching his shoulder. Tom Griffin had braced himself against the far side of the corridor and planted a mighty kick by the door handle, that put a hole in the door and cracked it open before he fell untidily to the floor.

She pushed through and was first inside. Pascal lay on the floor in the centre of the room. Blood was on his temple, on the floor and on a saxophone case not three feet away.

"Pascal!"

She dashed to him, crouched and felt his face. He groaned and recoiled but his eyes remained closed. The relief that he was alive turned quickly into shock that, for a moment, she had feared he was dead. She looked at the wound on his head. It was a shallow but long cut, bleeding freely.

"Pascal, can you hear me?"

There was movement at the door. She froze: Pascal's assailant might still be in here. But it was Tom, pushing aside the mess he'd made of the door, followed by Chaz Chase and the sound engineer, Tracy Chen.

"What in God's name's going on 'ere?" said Chaz, and then saw Pascal. "Hell!"

"Is he dead?" asked Tracy.

"Get a first aid kit," said Diana. "And call an ambulance."

She turned away and looked around the studio. In the midst of the refurbishments downstairs, this room had become a store room, a dumping ground. Boxes and equipment were piled up against the walls of the control room and the sound booth. An evening breeze blew in from the smashed window beside the fire exit door, bringing with it the sounds of the London evening.

She cradled Pascal's head in her hands and inspected his wound. His cheeks were warm beneath her hands. His lined skin was paler than she'd ever seen it.

"Who did this, Pascal? Pascal?"

He murmured and seemed to surface from a distant place. "Didn't... covered face..."

"Okay, okay. I need you to stay awake, my love."

He moaned and exhaled as though ready to drop off to sleep.

There was the tinkle of falling glass. Diana looked round to see Zaf standing outside the broken window on the fire escape. Bizarrely, he held a single brown shoe in one hand.

"Can you help them find a first aid kit?" she asked.

"But he's dead," said Zaf.

Diana frowned. "No, he's not."

Zaf nodded. He was pale. "He is."

"Who?"

"Paul. Paul Kensington."

She looked at him. What was he on about?

Zaf licked his lips. He blew out a breath and looked her in the eye. "Paul's dead."

Chapter Ten

Nothing killed a party quicker than the death of one guest and the injury of another.

Someone called the emergency services – Diana didn't know who – but there was an ambulance outside on Abbey Road within fifteen minutes, a minute earlier than the first police car.

While they waited, Tracy Chen found a first aid kit and pressed a dressing to Pascal's wound. Diana checked his pulse and talked to him throughout to stop him drifting off into unconsciousness. The paramedics came noisily up the stairs with their bulky packs on their backs. One immediately went back downstairs to fetch a body board to put Pascal on, and then the professionals took over.

Her hands coated in Pascal's blood, Diana allowed herself to be escorted downstairs. There were four police officers in the building by that time, and for reasons she really didn't care about and couldn't fathom anyway, Chaz Chase was having a stand-up row with one of them and Ernie was standing between them trying to take control of the situation.

A paramedic accompanied Ken, still cradling the shoulder he'd bashed against the studio door, out onto the pavement. Diana went with the other guests back into Studio One. The party food was still out on the low tables. Flutes of champagne stood undrunk on trays. Eighties synth music spilled out of the speakers.

"For God's sake," said Ariadne, sounding weary, "can someone turn that bloody music off?"

Someone did.

Zaf came in and headed straight for Diana.

"You OK?" he said.

"Compared to what?" she asked.

"Yeah. Point taken."

"I don't know if this is the kind of place I should be bringing Gus," said Newton, his voice faint, a faraway and horrified look in his eyes.

"I don't think it's like this all the time, mate," said Zaf. He put a hand on Newton's shoulder. "You look like you could do with a cup of tea, I reckon." He looked round at the catering options on offer.

"Maybe I can find a kettle somewhere," said Tom Griffin.

Chaz Chase and Ernie entered, Chaz grumbling bitterly, with a pair of police officers behind them. Two police detectives brought up the rear.

Diana knew both of them.

DCI Sugarbrook was a massive and muscular man, an ideal physique for a beat copper perhaps, but not what one would expect for the more esoteric business of criminal investigation. His colleague, DS Quigley, was a slender woman, smaller than her boss in whichever dimension you'd care to measure. Diana had found them both to be reasonable individuals, if occasionally lacking in the imagination and open-mindedness one might need to unpick a serious crime.

"Ladies and gentlemen," said Sugarbrook loudly, pushing back his long coat so he could put his hands in his trouser pockets, "I am Detective Chief Inspector Clint Sugarbrook of the London Metropolitan Police force. A serious incident has occurred in the building. I understand this may be unsettling, but I assure you that we are here to ensure everyone's safety and to get to the bottom of what happened. First and foremost, I ask for your full cooperation with our investigation, and would like you all to stay in this room while my colleagues check the building. One of my officers will come round and collect personal details from each of you. We will try to make this as quick as possible."

And with that, he departed.

"We're going to be here a long time," said Diana.

"Yeah?" said Tom.

"I need another drink," said Ariadne.

Diana looked at Zaf. "I think we should seek out that kettle. Teas all round."

Chapter Eleven

The police found a lounge to the rear of the building they could use as an interview space. Zaf was eventually called through and invited to sit in a cracked leather chair across a glass-topped coffee table from DCI Sugarbrook and DS Quigley. Sugarbrook nodded in recognition at Zaf.

His first question of note was, "You were outside on the fire escape, weren't you?"

"I was."

"Why?"

"We were trying to get into that studio on the second floor, and then we heard the window smash."

"Yes?"

"And because I'd been on that fire escape earlier I—"

"Why?"

"Why? Why was I on the fire escape? I was trying to get a phone signal."

"So, you thought, I'll go on the fire escape."

"Someone, um, Tracy the sound engineer, she told me that

it was best to go out there or up onto the roof if I wanted to use my phone."

"I see. Go on."

DS Quigley was making copious notes while Zaf spoke.

"So, I heard the window smash and I thought – I don't know why but I thought that whoever had attacked Pascal must have broken out and gone onto the fire escape. Or I guess it occurred to me that if we needed to get *in* to Pascal, I could do it by going down a floor, getting onto the fire escape, then going back up to the second and in that way. We were kinda keen to do something."

"And when you got onto the fire escape?" said Sugarbrook.

"That's when I heard the screams from below."

"Whose screams?"

"I dunno. I guess Ariadne Webb's. It was a high scream. It might have been Newton. I don't know. Not Ernie's, though he was down there."

"Ernie Holland was on the ground floor by the body?"

"Yes."

"But you didn't see Mr Kensington fall?"

Some part of Zaf wanted to say yes, even though it wasn't true. Some part of him wanted to say he had been there in Paul's final moments, and he wondered if it was because that way, he might somehow cling to some part of Paul, illogical though it sounded, or even try to save the man, even though he was a long way past saving.

"Did you see or hear him fall?" said Sugarbrook.

Zaf shook his head.

"So you have no idea exactly when Paul fell?"

"I heard the glass break. I ran. I..." He tried to mentally recreate his run down the stairs and out. "It can't have been more than thirty, forty seconds later."

DCI Sugarbrook nodded thoughtfully. "So, what do you think happened?"

"I've told you..."

"But what actually happened? In your understanding, what do you think occurred?"

"I've no idea why anyone would have locked themselves in the studio and attacked Pascal. Maybe someone objected to one of his restaurant reviews." He laughed, then immediately felt guilty and shut his mouth. "I don't know. I guess I thought that someone had attacked him, whacked him over the head and then gone out onto the fire escape and..." He shook his head. "Maybe the attacker bumped into Paul and perhaps in their blind panic to get away, pushed Paul over the side as they ran down."

"But you were out there thirty seconds after the window smashed."

"Maybe," said Zaf. "It's a guess. A person, a fast person, could have run to the bottom in that time. Hidden somewhere, or run away. Or even come in through that first floor fire exit and concealed themselves before I got there."

"But you didn't see anyone running away?"

Zaf considered. "No."

"But you saw three people on the ground." Sugarbrook peered over at Quigley's notes. "Big Ernie, Ariadne Webb and Newton Crombie."

"Correct."

"Any of them look out of breath to you?"

Zaf frowned. "You don't think any of them actually did it?"

"I don't know what to think yet, Mr Williams. There was no one on the first floor when you went down to go out?"

"No, but I think I heard people on the stairs. At least, I

knew that some people had heard the commotion and had come up very soon after."

"But you didn't actually see or hear them?"

Zaf had to interrogate his memory. It wasn't easy. "No. I don't think I did."

"Another question," said the detective chief inspector. "You saw Paul on the ground below, dead or dying, but you went *up* the stairs, yes?"

"I... did."

"Why?"

Zaf shook his head. "Because I had planned to go up? My brain was on autopilot, I suppose. I knew I had to reach Pascal. I'm not sure."

"But you did go up. Tell me about that."

Zaf took a deep breath.

"There was glass on the stairs. Lots of it. Some of it must have gone straight to the ground. Glass on the stairs and then I saw the shoe. It must have come off as Paul fell. Caught on something."

"So you went up to investigate. Potentially altering a crime scene."

Zaf looked down at his knees. "Sorry." He looked up again. "I was trying to help."

A grunt. "One last thing." Sugarbrook pulled a flat evidence bag from his inner pocket. He held it out to Zaf.

The bag held two large red bank notes. Zaf looked at it and then at Sugarbrook.

"Any comments?"

Zaf didn't know what he was asking. "They're fifty pound notes."

"Yes. Anything else?"

Zaf shrugged. "I never see fifty pound notes. Don't think

I've ever held one in my life. I thought only drug dealers and money launderers used them."

Sugarbrook gave him a questioning look. "Do you think Paul Kensington was involved in drugs or money laundering?"

Zaf pulled back a little. "Were these found on him? I... Drugs, no. He's the kind of man who'd call weed 'wacky-baccy'. Money laundering? He was an awful manager. I'm sorry, but he was. I don't think he'd have the, um, the intelligence to launder money. Is that a bad thing to say?"

Sugarbrook tapped the bag. "Anything interesting about the design?"

Zaf peered closer at the images on the bank note. "That's Sir John Houblon. First governor of the Bank of England. He was Lord Mayor of London too, I think."

"Very good knowledge," said DS Quigley.

"I'm a London tour guide," said Zaf, and then paused in thought. His boss was now dead.

"At least I was," he said.

Chapter Twelve

Diana was brought to the temporary interview room at the back of the building. DCI Sugarbrook was waiting for her.

"It is, once again, nice to speak to you, Miss Bakewell."

"It would be nice to meet under happier circumstances," she replied. "Did you leave me until last for a reason?"

"No reason."

Diana wasn't sure she believed him.

She'd sat in Studio One while guests and staff were called through one by one to give initial statements to the police. Most had not returned to the studio afterwards and, she supposed, had been allowed to leave.

DCI Sugarbrook sniffed. "I'm getting the impression that Paul Kensington was not a well-liked man."

"Life is full of all sorts of people," Diana replied.

"A bland sentiment, if you don't mind me saying. But he wasn't well-liked."

"Are you asking me if anyone disliked him enough to kill him?"

"Do you think anyone did?"

Diana gave it a moment's thought. Then she pushed it aside. "I had assumed you were working on the theory that Pascal Palmer was the attacker's target and that Paul was perhaps an innocent bystander, pushed to his death as the attacker fled the scene?"

Sugarbrook grunted. "We are not going to blind ourselves to any possibilities."

"Have you considered the idea that it was Paul who attacked Pascal, before breaking out through the window and then falling accidentally to his death? That would be a neat little theory requiring no additional elements."

DS Quigley underlined something in her notebook.

"Your tone of voice suggests you don't think that likely," said Sugarbrook.

Diana was surprised at his perceptiveness.

"No. I don't think Paul was Pascal's attacker. For several reasons."

"Please. Do tell."

"Firstly, Paul is not a very physical man. Pascal might be nearly seventy but he's always been a tall and powerful person. Paul was, to be frank, a weedy individual. And a coward to boot. I don't have a problem with physical cowardice as a rule. Violence is abhorrent. Paul might have been a petty, stupid, grudge-bearing individual, but he wasn't a brute. Secondly, those of us who were there outside the door heard the attacker speak."

DS Quigley flicked back through her notes. "Tom Griffin, Ken Ferrari and Zaf Williams."

"Yes. I think so."

"You know so," said Sugarbrook with a half-smile.

"I do. We heard the attacker speak. It was muffled. It was

through the door. It could conceivably have been male or female, a middling voice, but it was a London accent. Paul spoke BBC English and, well, his most convincing London accent would have sounded very much like Dick Van Dyke in Mary Poppins."

"So, a Londoner. East End?"

Diana wanted to nod, but couldn't. "Maybe. A bit of an Estuary accent, nothing either of you couldn't muster if you wanted to sound rough and threatening. Also, there was the matter of the mask."

"What mask?" said Sugarbrook.

"Or balaclava. I don't know. When Tom managed to break in, I got to Pascal first. He was delirious but he said something about the attacker's face being covered. I should guess that if Paul had been wearing or carrying some obvious face covering, you'd have found it somewhere on the ground by now."

Sugarbrook's head tilt was as much acknowledgement as he was going to give. "It sounds like you saw and heard a lot."

"Several of us were on the stairs below when we heard the shouts and the scuffle. It was more noise than anything else."

"But you heard a voice. What did it say?"

"'Give it to me' or something very much like that." Diana strove to be precise. "The voice was insistent and demanding."

"Give what?" said Quigley.

Diana looked at her. "I've no idea. Pascal was saying 'who are you?' and 'what do you want?'. More than once."

"He didn't know his attacker?"

"Or didn't recognise them. He was alarmed. Maybe some bravado." She remembered the blood, on the floor and on the instrument case. Internally she winced. "How is he?"

DCI Sugarbrook met her gaze.

"Both Mr Palmer and Mr Ferrari have been taken to the

Royal Free Hospital. Ken Ferrari has a suspected shoulder fracture. Pascal appears to have concussion and they're monitoring him. He's..." He mushed his lips thoughtfully. "Head injuries are difficult to assess. He's not a young man."

"Is he in danger?"

"They're just monitoring him. When we're done, we can see if anyone will be permitted to see him. He doesn't have close family?"

"No. There's family elsewhere, but no."

"He and Ariadne Webb were a couple once, correct?"

"Yes, but not for a long time. It was an acrimonious split."

"And they're not on speaking terms?"

Diana gave him a piercing look. "Are you looking for a motive?"

"Ariadne Webb. Where was she when all this was happening?"

"She went downstairs for a refill of champagne," Diana told him.

"And who else was with you? Or not with you?"

Diana swallowed. "Tom and Ken were with me at the moment we got into Studio Three. Zaf had run downstairs to try to get back up there via the fire escape. Chaz and Tracy Chen were there moments later."

"How much later?"

"No time at all. They must have heard the commotion."

"So they were on the first or second floor?"

Diana hesitated. "You would like me to speculate on where they might have been? It's two flights of stairs. They could have been on the ground floor when the shouting started. I didn't see them. I don't know." She mentally checked what she'd said. "That's it. That's all the people I can account for, before or after. You think it had to be someone already in the building?"

"We're ruling nothing in and nothing out at this time," said Sugarbrook. He hesitated, then added, "Oh," as though he'd forgotten something. He put a clear plastic bag in front of her. It contained two fifty pound notes.

"What are these?" she said.

"I had hoped you were more astute than that, Miss Bakewell."

"I mean, where did you find them?"

"Hanging halfway out of Paul Kensington's jacket pocket. Note anything unusual?"

"They're Sir John Houblon fifty pound notes."

"They are."

"He was governor of the Bank of England, Lord Mayor of London, and the Master of the Worshipful Company of Grocers from 1690 to 1691."

"Very good."

"But what's perhaps most interesting about these banknotes," she continued, "is that they've not been legal tender in the UK since twenty-fourteen."

"Ah." Sugarbrook had apparently got the answer he had been waiting for.

"And you're wondering why Paul Kensington was walking around with a hundred quid in banknotes that haven't been legal usable tender for a decade."

"One of many questions."

Chapter Thirteen

The police asked Diana if she would be able to get herself home. In truth, she needed the walk and she wasn't sure she even wanted to go home. The events of the evening swirled around her head. Some she could not let go of, and others would not let go of her.

Though Diana loved walking, her temporary but increasingly permanent home in her mum's flat in Bromley-by-Bow was eight miles away and too far to walk in the deepening evening. But the forty minute tube ride from St John's Wood to West Ham gave her time to try to settle her mind.

Nonetheless, once she was home, she was in no mood to talk. She found her mum, Beverley, gave her a brief and honest account of the evening and then, with apologies, retired to bed where sleep eluded her for many hours.

The following morning, a Saturday, Diana made her way to the Chartwell and Crouch depot on Chiltern Street. She asked herself why she had gone there rather than staying at her mum's place, and the answer she gave herself was that she felt a strong sense of responsibility.

Paul Kensington was dead. She was the most senior member of staff after Paul, so within their little workplace things would need taking care of. What that meant exactly, she wasn't sure.

She also needed to do something with her day or else she would just dwell on unhelpful things like Pascal Palmer's injuries. She'd phoned the Royal Free Hospital first thing, but had simply been told that he was 'resting' and not receiving any visitors. When asked if she was family, her first instinct had been to point out that Pascal really had nothing in the way of family, and that she was among the few people in the world who knew him well enough to care. But she kept her thoughts to herself. It didn't work like that, she knew.

When she arrived at the bus depot, she found Zaf and Newton in the kitchen, drinking tea in silence. They too had been drawn here, despite the fact that they had no work on today. Gus slumbered on Newton's lap, sensing the sombre mood.

"What happens now?" asked Newton.

Diana pulled up a chair and joined them. "I'm about to try and find out."

Newton and Zaf looked at her with watery smiles. If she could achieve nothing else, at least she could attempt to salvage staff morale. She drank a cup of tea with them while they all attempted to make sense of the situation.

"Alexsei had come down to Abbey Road to meet me," Zaf said, unprompted. "Poor guy spent two hours standing on the pavement wondering what the hell was going on. He was shocked of course, when I was able to tell him."

"Did you tell your family what happened, Newton?" asked Diana. Newton had a wife and many children at home, though he rarely mentioned them. His workplace persona was focused one hundred percent on buses, as well as a certain grey tabby cat.

Newton shook his head. "I couldn't imagine what I could tell them. There's enough to worry about, isn't there? Our jobs, for one."

Diana nodded gravely. Eventually she stood, knowing she had to go into Paul Kensington's office and take a look around.

She sat in his chair, taking stock of the space in a way she'd never needed to before. Paul hadn't kept much paper in his office, which meant she needed access to his computer.

The box of paper and office oddments he'd been sorting through in the last week of his life still sat partially unsorted on his desk. The stuff inside looked years old. Chartwell and Crouch was full of little cupboards and drawers and secret spaces. There was one cupboard, which they occasionally tried to board up, leading to a little warren of tiny tunnels that connected eventually with the tube line from Baker Street. They knew this because cats had come through it from time to time, including a violent, spitting, yowling monster called Boudicca. There was a whole secret floor in the upper reaches of the depot building where Newton had constructed various models of London landmarks. Given enough time (which they certainly did not have) he might have turned the whole floor into a secret model village of the entire city.

But, if Diana was to do anything practical today, she wasn't going to need the forgotten records of the past. She needed access to current work materials. What little work Paul Kensington had done to support the company involved his computer.

She powered up his laptop and stared at the login screen. She would need his password, of course. Had he kept a note of it?

Probably not.

Still, she had to look. She pulled open drawers, and checked underneath the keyboard and mouse mat for stickers, but there were none. She found a banana in a drawer, and removed it. A snack that he would never have a chance to eat.

Diana sighed and wondered if she could guess Paul's password. What did she really know about the man who had been her boss?

She carried on going through Paul's drawers and the small cupboard that sat against the side wall. There were brochures from competitors and samples of merchandise from promotional companies, but there was very little that spoke of Paul the man, rather than Paul the manager at Chartwell and Crouch.

She came across a pile of leaflets for the Londiniumarium and placed them on the desk, suddenly thoughtful. The Londiniumarium had been the closest thing Paul had to a passion project. It was a terrible idea, to crowbar all of London's sights, sounds and culture into a tacky warehouse, but he'd been convinced it was the future. Diana wasn't even sure whether it was still open. She'd never seen any write-ups or heard any recommendations for it. Truth was, she'd been embarrassed to be associated with it.

An idea crossed her mind. She sat at the computer and tried *Londiniumarium* as the password.

The screen changed, opening up to Paul's desktop. She was in.

Over the next two hours, Diana made a list of Paul's business contacts that she'd need to inform of his passing, and tackled the upcoming meetings on his calendar. Those seemed like the most urgent tasks, so now she could afford to slow down and try to work out the general state of the business.

As she browsed the folders on his computer, she became curious to know what he'd done with the business plan she'd sent him. She ran a search for the title of the document and found nothing. He hadn't stored it anywhere. She went to his email to find out whether he'd filed it in there, but when she searched for the original email she found it in the trash. Had he even read it?

Diana doubted it. It felt wrong to be angry with someone who'd been so casually murdered just the day before, but Diana couldn't help herself.

She took a deep breath and resolved to rise above her anger. While she'd been searching for her document she had found a folder that seemed to contain Paul's plans for Chartwell and Crouch. That would be as good a place to start as any.

She went and grabbed another cup of tea, and settled in to read the documents that would determine their future.

Chapter Fourteen

B y noon, Zaf had had a bellyful of tea. He felt the urge to move, but didn't know what to do.

"Hey, Newton. How's the prep going for Gus's recording career?" he asked.

Diana, sitting at the kitchen table with Paul's laptop, raised her eyebrows.

Newton looked up with a frown. "Recording career?"

Zaf tried a smile. "I thought Ken Ferrari was keen to get Gus in to be part of his cat concerto or whatever." He felt his smile falter. "Or has this, um, nasty business put a stop to that?"

Newton dug his phone out of his pocket. "I've actually had a message from Ken. He was released from hospital late last night with a fractured collarbone, and he's been in contact several times since."

"Really?"

A nod. "He's very keen." Newton gave his cat a stroke and Gus lifted his head. Newton smiled. "Gus will be a natural."

"No prep needed, then."

"He might need a little conditioning, if we want him to miaow on cue."

Newton stood up, placed Gus on the seat of the chair and left the room. He returned with a packet of treats and a catnip mouse.

Gus sniffed the air. He knew immediately that Newton had something interesting, and he sat up straight.

"How do you intend to do this?" asked Zaf. "Cats are well known for being untrainable."

"I'm not sure that's true," Newton replied. "Positive reinforcement can work on cats. I just need to make sure that I reward Gus when he does what I want."

Zaf watched Newton as he crouched in front of Gus.

"Miaow!" said Newton. "Miaow!" He paused, waiting for Gus to respond.

Gus tilted his head and looked at Newton.

"Miaow!" said Newton. "Miaow."

Gus emitted the smallest sound. At a stretch, it might, just possibly, have been a 'Miaow'.

"Good boy, Gus!" Newton gave him a treat. He grinned at Zaf.

Zaf had to hand it to Newton. He did nothing by halves, and at least his mind was no longer dwelling on the demise of their boss.

Newton tickled Gus's ears and looked thoughtful. "I wonder if there are ways to encourage him to sing? What d'you reckon, Gus?"

"Cats aren't known for being easy to train," said Diana.

"Not all cats are as smart as Gus," said Newton. He looked intently at Gus. "Miaow!"

They all stared at Gus, wondering if he'd answer, but Gus acted as if he hadn't heard.

"Miaow!" said Zaf, reaching over to stroke the cat. "Come on Gus, miaow!"

Gus emitted a small, dismissive sound that sounded more like 'meh'. They all burst out laughing.

"I think you must have said something that didn't translate well!" said Diana. "Probably need to brush up on your miaowing, both of you."

"Yes. I can work on that," said Newton. Zaf looked up and met Diana's eye. They both knew he was being deadly serious.

Chapter Fifteen

The next day, Diana received a message from Ernie, suggesting a catch up. On Monday morning, after making all the necessary phone calls she could regarding Paul Kensington, she messaged him back to arrange a rendezvous.

She was grateful for the change of scenery.

Ernie was being fitted for a new suit at his Mayfair tailors and had suggested that they meet afterwards, but Diana enjoyed the chance to poke around the rarified corners of London, and Savile Row was no exception. Ernie's tailor was in a grand old building, rich with wood and gilt decoration. Diana dawdled in the front of the shop, examining samples of fine wool fabric that came in endless variations of colour and pattern. There was a comfortable chair for her to relax in while she waited for Ernie to emerge from the fitting rooms.

"Will I get to see your new suit?" she asked.

Ernie shook his head. "First fitting today. They have to take their time, don't they? Be a few weeks I reckon. How you holding up, dear?"

"I'm fine," she said. "How are you holding up?"

He nodded. "Now, let's take a wander through Burlington Arcade and head to Piccadilly, eh? I'm in the mood fer a bit of posh. Savile Row'll do that to yer!"

Diana smiled as she walked arm-in-arm with Ernie. She pointed up to the blue plaque that marked the location of the Beatles rooftop performance as they passed number three Savile Row. "It would have been a thing to see that, wouldn't it?"

"I saw it," Ernie told her.

"No! Really? You never said."

Ernie nodded. "Back in those days I was an errand boy fer my uncle Mostie. He had me all over the place, cos of my young legs. A mate over in Soho told me to get over here, said the Beatles were playing fer free. Course, I didn't believe him but I knew I'd kick meself if it turned out to be true." Ernie made an expansive gesture. "He was right, weren't he?"

Diana smiled.

They turned the corner and entered the glorious covered Burlington Arcade with its timeless row of luxury shops. Ernie's expression darkened. "However used you get to violence, that was a nasty business on Friday."

"It was. Puts everything in perspective. Before that happened I'd been wrapped up in other worries and then – wallop – this. Now all those troubles seem so far away. I don't know if the police have any idea who did it."

"A little bird tells me they're working on the theory that it was a burglar surprised in the act by Pascal."

"Really?"

"Maybe because of the balaclava thing. Maybe because they can't work out why anyone would want to attack Pascal."

"And then this burglar flew down the fire escape and

vanished into nowhere?" Diana shook her head. "It's a stretch. They'll still need to find out who this nowhere man is."

"Ah, well," said Ernie with a wry smile at the reference. "I heard a little something on the grapevine. Apparently the police nicked Maxwell Best last night not far from Abbey Road."

Diana didn't recognise the name.

"He's what the police would probably call a 'prime suspect'," said Ernie, miming the air quotes with his one free hand, "on account of him having a history of aggravated assault and burglary."

"Oh really? Well that sounds like it's definitely a lead."

"Yeah, yeah. The coppers must be relieved. I'm not sure Maxwell was doing anything other than drinking in the wrong boozer at the wrong time, though. We'll see how it pans out, eh?"

Diana shrugged. It was good to know that the police were taking action, even if Ernie was sceptical. In his line of work, he was hardly likely to be a fan of the thin blue line.

"How's Chaz doing?" she asked. "It was a shame that his launch party was messed up like that."

Ernie paused to look at a display of gloves. They were expensive leather gloves, artfully placed in old-fashioned jars in an eye-catching array of colours.

"Nice display, that," he said. "Like the old sweet shops. Chaz? He's still in the honeymoon period with his recording studio and this Lamé Records business, so nuffin's gonna spoil that fer 'im. Know what he called me about earlier? He'd been through Baker Street tube station and he was raving about some cat he saw down there. A potential contributor to Ken Ferrari's mad album of cat music. Look, he's sent me this video."

Ernie fiddled with his phone, then held it out for Diana to see. Chaz had captured shaky video footage on the Bakerloo platform at Baker Street. It featured a slightly out-of-focus cat, sitting on top of an electricity junction box, about six feet up the wall, and yowling at passers-by like a furry busker with a bad attitude.

Diana laughed. "Good lord, that's Boudicca!"

Ernie lowered his phone. "Yer not telling me you recognise this cat? It's not even in focus."

"Boudicca is quite the character. She lived in the depot for a while, but if I recall correctly, she escaped by chewing her way through solid concrete. I never met a scarier cat."

"Well, I better let Chaz know. He showed this to Ken and now Ken's totally smitten with yer Boudicca, has some fantasy about her being the star of his cat album. I mean, the gel's got a set of pipes on 'er, ain't she?"

"She is quite vocal," Diana agreed. "But I thought Gus was going to be the star of the album."

"The music business is a fickle thing, ain't it?"

She shrugged. "Nonetheless, I suppose it's possible that Newton and Zaf could persuade her out of hiding. I'll ask them. I don't think we can make any promises to Chaz, but it would do the boys good to have a distraction."

"I gotcha," said Ernie, tapping the side of his nose. "Say the word if you need any help from me, like tranks or whatever."

"Tranquilisers?" She gave him a look. "Where on earth would you get those from?"

The old gangster tapped the side of his nose again. "Trust your Uncle Ernie. He can lay his hands on all sorts."

Chapter Sixteen

When Diana got back to the depot she found Zaf and Newton absorbed in some kind of game with Gus.

"If I didn't know better I'd say you were trying to train that cat to sing," she said.

"It's working!" Newton told her. "Listen." He had a tiny glockenspiel, which looked like a child's toy. He hit one of the bars with the little wooden hammer and as it rang out, he echoed the note with his own voice. "Miaowww!"

Zaf held a treat at the ready, as the three humans eyed Gus.

Gus seemed amused by all the attention. Eventually he emitted a brief sound. "Miaow."

"See! He's a natural!" Newton said.

Zaf and Newton exchanged a high five.

"Well, I'm glad you've found something to do," said Diana. "I might have something else for you."

Zaf frowned. "Have you figured out what we're all supposed to be doing yet? Do you know what state the business is in?"

"No." Diana hadn't finished digging yet, and thought it better to keep the little she had found to herself. "Surprisingly, it's a task that's related to the one you're currently engaged in."

Newton and Zaf both peered at her in surprise.

"Do either of you remember Boudicca?" she asked.

Newton scowled. "Boudicca who managed to bite me even through leather gloves? Boudicca who chewed her way to freedom through the wall?"

"Boudicca whose owner we tracked down but who definitely didn't want her back?" Zaf added.

"The very one." Diana smiled. "It seems that she has taken to yowling at passengers in Baker Street underground station."

"Oh no!" said Newton. "Has someone set the feds on her?"

Diana frowned. "Not as far as I know, but Chaz saw her. He would like her to take part in his recording project. I wondered if the two of you might want to try to recapture her and take her along?"

Newton and Zaf exchanged a look, excitement mingled with more than a little fear.

"We need to make a list," said Newton. "Welding gauntlets, a reinforced cat carrier and lots of fresh sardines."

"Does it have to be sardines?" Zaf asked.

"It was sardines that brought her here in the first place."

Gus miaowed loudly, making everyone jump.

"I think Gus has concerns," said Zaf. "What is it, Gus? Are you worried about Boudicca? D'you think she might hurt us?"

"If I had to hazard a guess," said Diana, "it would be that you used a word he understood. Sardines."

Gus miaowed loudly again.

"Well I never!" said Newton. "That might be useful for getting Gus to sing. I think we've killed two birds with one stone."

Chapter Seventeen

That evening Diana sat with her mum Beverley, in the flat near one of the many waterways that met in the East End.

Beverley was working on a jigsaw of an old fashioned shop window. She'd decided that it was the Old Curiosity Shop and so had chosen to accompany it with the audiobook of the Dickens classic. The routine of jigsaws and thematically linked audiobooks was something that Beverley enjoyed, but Diana had found it difficult to insert herself into a daily life that was so insular.

Her mum was an active and sociable woman, especially for someone in her eighties, but she did like her small homely pleasures. Diana, by contrast, preferred an almost exclusively outdoor existence, of strolling the streets, of chatting with acquaintances new and old.

After finally summoning the courage to explain that she found afternoons and evenings like these annoying, Diana had suggested a compromise. Beverley would pause the audiobook for at least half an hour so that they could chat. It made things a little more companiable.

"Lamp, lamp, lamp, lamp." Beverley scoured the remaining pieces, the box lid in her hand. "You know, I knew little Maxwell Best when he was a lad."

"The burglar they've arrested?" said Diana, surprised.

Beverly nodded. "It's our Rita's neighbour's sister's boy. An unpleasant little toerag, to be certain."

"Well, he's behind bars now."

Beverley grunted. "Oh, if he killed that Paul Kensington chap then I'm Charley's Aunt. You know the Old Bill. When they don't know who's responsible for something they just go and pick up a few likely subjects. Days were, when if you were London Irish, you couldn't walk down the street without getting nicked and fitted up for some crime or other."

Diana wanted to argue with her and explain that the Metropolitan Police had come a long way in the last fifty years. But she didn't disagree with her mum's assessment that the attacks on Pascal and Paul were something other than a burglary gone wrong.

"I don't know if the police will ever get to the bottom of it," she said. "It's unfathomable why anyone would wish Pascal harm. He's a food writer, mostly retired now, a man of a certain age. I'm not aware he's got any enemies."

"Certain restaurant owners?" suggested Beverley.

"You're not the first to suggest that, even in jest. And with Pascal in hospital, I'm not going to hear his side of the story for a while."

Beverley was frowning at the pieces on the table in her search for the lamp.

"Him and Ariadne Webb aren't on good terms," she said.

"If she was going to hurt him, she would have done it years ago."

Beverley grunted. "Theirs was a tempestuous relationship. How's your Zaf holding up after this rum to-do? He's a delicate sort, I always feel."

Diana laughed at that. "He might look like he'd blow over in a stiff breeze but our Zaf has an inner steel. I should think he's doing fine."

"He needs feeding up, that lad does."

"He does not. He's happy as he is and I should imagine Alexsei is looking after him well enough."

Beverley murmured doubtfully. "I don't see how you can be happy with Zaf shacked up with the son of the man who tossed you out of your home."

"The behaviour of rich men like Kamran Dadashov is perhaps beyond our understanding, Mum. But Alexsei has severed almost all ties with his dad. Wise or not, Alexsei's loyalties lie with Zaf now."

The owner of the Eccleston Square house where Diana had lived for decades had turfed her out by exploiting the smallest of technical discrepancies in her old rent agreement. Diana still smarted at this hostile action, but she tried to remind herself that she had been able to live in a large and stylish London town house for decades with a ridiculously low rent. She should be grateful for the time she'd had there.

"What's done is done," she said. "I am throwing myself into things that I can have some small control over."

"Oh, yes?"

"Firstly, keeping the depot running. There's a woman from head office, Rita something, coming over to inspect things. If there's any hope for our little outpost then I need to show her that we're a viable prospect."

"Uh-huh?"

"Secondly, I've not yet given up on Morris Walker."

"Now, there's a lost cause," said Beverley.

"You think he defrauded Chartwell and Crouch for millions with a fake ticket scam?"

"What I think doesn't matter, does it? But the courts found him guilty and they don't tend to change their minds."

Diana shook her head. "His alibi for the time when the cash was being withdrawn from the bank was a little café."

"Where no one remembers seeing him."

"Except he mentioned an old woman with a Pomeranian."

"Marengo. This mysterious Marengo that's going to be the star witness that proves his innocence."

"Zaf swears he saw an older woman near Sloane Square, calling 'Marengo, Marengo' to her little dog."

Her mum shook her head. "Slender hope there, Diana love. Slender hope."

Diana bristled. "We do what we can for who we can. Unless you'd like to offer some of your wisdom on the matter?"

Beverley shrugged and picked up her ancient hifi's remote control to turn the audiobook back on.

"Oh!" she exclaimed.

"An idea?" said Diana.

"There it is!" Beverley pointed. "The lamp bit. It's right by your hand. Pass it to me."

Chapter Eighteen

On Tuesday morning, Zaf and Newton made their way to Baker Street station. Zaf carried the bag of supplies and Newton had the bulky cat carrier. Baker Street underground was a mere five minute walk from the bus depot.

"If Boudicca found her way into the underground from the bottom of that cupboard," said Newton, "do you think she's been living in tunnels ever since she left us?"

"I'm not sure," replied Zaf. "It makes her sound like something from a horror film. Boudicca the underground cat who hasn't seen daylight for over a year. Eats rats and terrorises tube passengers."

Newton smiled. "I'm quite looking forward to seeing her again."

"We'll have to find her first," said Zaf. "Baker Street has several platforms."

"Ten. More underground platforms than any other station."

Zaf smiled. Newton wasn't a tour guide in the same way

that Zaf and Diana were, but his knowledge of arcane London trivia never ceased to amaze. There was a special flavour of geeky, Newton-style trivia that he excelled at.

"Well, according to what Diana said, it was the Bakerloo line where she was seen, so let's try there first."

They descended into the deeper parts of the station and made their way along the platform.

Newton turned to Zaf. "How well do you know Ariadne?"

The question took him aback. "I've met her a few times. I wouldn't say I know her well, though. She spends all her time messing with Diana. The two of them trade these barbed insults. Why do you ask?"

Newton shrugged. "She was married to that Pascal who got hurt. It's nearly always the spouse, or ex-spouse, isn't it? I bet the police are looking at her."

Newton probably had a point. "Maybe," Zaf replied. "The thing is, if you've already split up with a person who caused you pain, why wouldn't you just leave them well alone?"

Newton tapped the side of his nose. "Ah, well, that's why I think it's clever. If I wanted to murder my wife, and I don't by the way, but if I did, I would do exactly that. You ignore them for years then pounce when they least expect it. Who's going to believe that I'd wait that long?"

"Well, the police, according to what you just said," said Zaf.

"Maybe. I still think it would be the clever, sneaky way to do it."

"Well, Ariadne is clever," said Zaf. "I think that's why she annoys Diana so much. She's smart and efficient. The two of them should really be friends. They used to be, apparently."

"Yeah. People." Newton shook his head. "It's just..."

"It's just what?" said Zaf.

Newton sighed. "When we heard the ruckus at the recording studio the other day, we rushed outside, that Ernie Holland and me. Went out to the back yard where the noises seemed to be coming from and where... well, where Paul was found."

"It must have been horrible to see."

"The thing is, Ariadne was already there. Like..." Newton reached out a hand, as though to grasp the remembered scene. "We came through the door, the bottom of the fire escape stairs was over there. And Ariadne too. She could have gone through the door ahead of us. She could equally have come down the stairs."

"You're saying you saw her come down the fire escape."

"I said no such thing, Zaf. What I'm saying is I don't know where she did come from. It's concerning."

"Did you tell the police?"

Newton nodded.

"Well, that's that, then," said Zaf. They reached the far end of the platform and Zaf pointed at the wall. "Look, that's where she was sitting in the video."

"Do you think she'll remember us?"

Zaf considered. "She might remember that we fed her well, yeah." Was Newton expecting the cat to bear a grudge against the person who had locked her in the stationery cupboard?

"Let's try the sardines then, shall we?" Newton said.

They found a bench and set down the cat carrier. Zaf opened the bag.

"We've got sardines, catnip and the glockenspiel." He looked up at Newton. "What were we going to do with the glockenspiel again?"

"You saw how Gus was. Maybe Boudicca'll enjoy the sound too."

Zaf had seen no real evidence that Gus enjoyed the sound of the glockenspiel. The cat just liked being the centre of attention. He shrugged and placed the little instrument onto the bench. Newton tapped it experimentally.

"Play *Three Blind Mice*," suggested Zaf.

Newton picked out the tune with the little hammer. A tube train arrived and passengers got out. One of them threw a twenty pence coin towards Newton.

"Thank you," he said without looking up. He played the tune again.

The platform grew quiet.

"I'm going to take a sardine and walk up and down the platform," said Newton. "We need to give her a chance to smell it."

Zaf nodded.

Newton picked up a sardine then shrugged and picked up another. He held one in each hand, above his head. He walked the length of the platform, ignoring the knots of people who paused ever so briefly in their bustling commute, to wonder what he was up to.

"Smile!" said Zaf as Newton walked back towards him. He took a photo.

"What are you doing?"

"Some things just need to be documented, Newton. I'm sending it to Diana as an update. I might also be sending it to Alexsei, inviting him to invent a caption."

Newton tutted and rolled his eyes. "I might as well do another circuit."

"Might as well," agreed Zaf. He bent over his phone, tittering as he sent the picture.

Newton clattered back towards him. "Gauntlets! Open the cage! Action stations!"

Zaf looked up as a shadow moved along the platform.

There was an unmistakeable feline fluidity as it nipped between people's legs and jumped up to trot along a bench.

"Come on!" Newton hissed. "We have to be ready."

Zaf made sure that the door to the carrier was open and that it was set for easy access. They both pulled on the enormous leather gauntlets as Boudicca approached.

"The fish! Pick it up!" Newton said. "Otherwise she'll just grab it and run off."

Both Newton and Zaf tried to pick up a sardine with the thick gloves on, but they were unable to get a grip on the slippery scales.

"I can't!" Zaf said. "Not with these on."

He pulled off a glove, planning to pick up the fish with his free hand and place it in the other, gloved hand. But by the time he'd grabbed the fish, Boudicca had it clamped firmly in her jaws.

Zaf held onto the fish, hoping the cat would let go.

But this was Boudicca.

He stood holding the sardine while she met his gaze with her murderous glare. She seemed to be daring him to try and take the fish from her.

"It's your fish, Boudicca," he said. "I'm not going to take it off you, honest."

She responded with a look of pure malevolence, almost as if she was trying mind control on him.

Could cats do that?

He saw a small movement in his peripheral vision and realised that Newton had got hold of the cat carrier and was bringing it up underneath. Zaf held his breath. If Boudicca realised what was about to happen she might just decide to drop the sardine and exact her own bloody revenge.

"Let go now," said Newton softly, and Zaf released the

sardine. Boudicca tumbled into the upended cat carrier and Newton slammed the door shut.

"Whatever you do, don't let the door open while I secure it," said Newton.

Zaf looked down in horror, seeing what he needed to do. "I can't put my hand in front of the door! She'll tear me apart!"

The door was a grill, with gaps wide enough for a cat's paws to extend out.

Zaf slapped his gauntleted hand on the door to keep it shut. He could feel the onslaught of Boudicca's angry attack. How long would it take her to get through the leather? Her claws raked across the surface, pulling shreds away. Her face was pressed up against the grill too, and Zaf could feel her teeth as they sank into the gauntlet.

"Nearly got the top and bottom catches done," grunted Newton. "There!"

They both stood back and looked at the carrier.

Zaf stooped down and peered inside. "Hey, Boudicca! Remember us?"

The cat flung herself at the door of the cage with an angry hiss, making Zaf topple over backwards with shock. Newton laughed.

"Not funny," said Zaf, then looked up and saw Newton's phone pointing at him.

"Oh, it was quite funny," said Newton. He took another picture of Zaf with a grin. "Just documenting things."

Chapter Nineteen

Diana was in Paul Kensington's office when Zaf and Newton returned to the depot. She sat at the desk, looking at the screen, deep in concentration.

"Did you find her?" she asked.

Newton proudly held up the cat carrier. "You should have seen our amazing teamwork."

"So what do you plan to do with her now?" asked Diana. "When does Ken want you to bring her to the studio?"

"This evening," said Zaf.

Diana turned in the swivel chair. "Well, you can't leave her in the carrier until this evening."

Zaf and Newton looked at each other. Neither of them had actually believed that they would get this far.

"If we let her out she might attack Gus," said Newton. "What do we do?"

After a long pause during which nobody had any sensible suggestions, Diana sighed. "The most obvious answer is this room. We can shut the door. She'll be safe in here."

Zaf and Newton nodded quietly. Nobody wanted to point

out that it would have been impossible when Paul Kensington was alive.

"There's even a litter tray in here," said Newton. He pointed at Paul Kensington's weird little Japanese sand garden in the corner.

Diana looked as if she was about to disagree, but she simply shrugged. "She might as well make use of it."

Newton bustled about getting things ready for Boudicca's stay. He set out a pair of bowls, with food and fresh water. He put one of his old sweaters into a cardboard box so she could have a comfy bed.

Meanwhile Diana made sure that the room was emptied of Paul Kensington's things, although there didn't seem to be much of them about.

"I think we're ready to release her from the carrier," said Newton. "Everyone out."

He placed the carrier near to the door of the office, loosened the catches that held it closed and then darted out of the door.

The three of them crowded around the glass window to watch Boudicca emerge from the carrier. She seemed to sense that they were there, turning to hiss at the door. She stalked around the space, trotting over every surface and sniffing to see what she could find. She examined the sand of Paul's garden, dabbing it lightly with a paw.

"Do you think she'll have a nap in the box?" Newton asked. "Gus loves a cardboard box."

Boudicca passed the box with barely a sideways glance, before climbing into Paul Kensington's chair. She raked her claws across both of the arms, making foam emerge from the parallel rips. Satisfied with her work, she sat on the chair as if she was waiting for someone to return the laptop so she could get her work done.

"We need to see if we can get her to sing," said Newton. "I'll get the glockenspiel."

Diana left to continue her work, but Zaf couldn't miss this.

Newton returned with the glockenspiel. "I'll play, you watch what she does," he instructed Zaf.

Newton tapped out the tune to *Three Blind Mice* once more.

Zaf watched carefully but Boudicca didn't even seem to register the sound. "She didn't move a muscle."

"Well we need to find something else then," said Newton. "Let's try singing to her, shall we? Do you want to go first?"

"Absolutely not," said Zaf.

Newton rolled his eyes. "Fine. What shall we try? I'll do *Bat Out of Hell*."

Newton started to sing the old Meatloaf song. Zaf wondered whether it was a karaoke favourite. Newton seemed to realise that it was a very long song, and stopped before he'd got halfway.

"No response there."

Zaf tried not to meet Newton's eye, as he knew he'd be expected to sing.

"Go on then, your turn."

Zaf huffed. "Shall we try some Abba? Everyone loves Abba. I'll do *Dancing Queen*."

Zaf launched into the song, which was punctuated with enough elongated *oooh* sounds that he felt he could properly go to town on the delivery. Of course, Boudicca couldn't see his dance moves, but he did them anyway.

"Nice job," said Newton when he'd finished. "No response, though."

Zaf massaged his throat. "Hard work that. I could never be

a professional singer." He laughed. "Of course, we do have a professional singer here in the depot. Why didn't we think of it before? We should get Diana to sing."

Zaf went to the kitchenette, where Diana had set up her temporary desk on a table. "Hey, Diana, you'll never guess what we're doing?"

"Are you singing for that cat? I can hear you in here, you know. In fact, I could almost see you, too. Were you doing the dance moves by any chance?"

Zaf felt his cheeks redden. "Maybe. We haven't got any reaction from her yet. We wondered if you'd have a go?"

Diana sighed wearily. Zaf knew that she had a lot on her plate.

"Listen, don't worry, we'll keep trying, you've got enough to do with working out what's going on with the business."

"Have you thought about the ambient sounds of the underground?" Diana asked. "If she was responding to something in the tube station it was more likely to be the noises around her than Abba or Meatloaf."

"Oh yeah! That's a good idea."

Zaf went back round to join Newton outside the office. "Let's try sound effects. I'm just trying to find some."

"Oh right. I've got loads of those," said Newton.

"You have? How come?"

"I like them," said Newton with a shrug. "Do we want crowd sounds or the specifics of a tube train?"

"Mate, this is your speciality," said Zaf. "Take it away,"

Newton tapped on his phone. "I've got a tube journey playlist. Here we go."

Zaf marvelled as Newton played the sounds of the London Underground. There was the odd whumpf of air as a train arrived through the tunnel, the sound of its brakes, and then the doors. There was the rhythmic clatter of it pulling away and that unearthly screaming sound that the trains sometimes made. Zaf was about to ask Newton what caused the noise when they both saw Boudicca raise her head like a howling wolf.

"Yowww!" echoed powerfully through the depot.

"That cat can sustain a note," said Newton, with a nod of admiration.

Chapter Twenty

In the kitchen, the three Chartwell and Crouch employees sat together and shared a pot of tea. Gus paraded around, tail high, unimpressed that another feline had been brought into his domain.

"If you're going to be a recording star, you'll have to learn how to play nice with others," Newton told him.

Zaf helped himself to a chocolate biscuit from the tin on the table. "So, how are things with the business? Merely awful, or so bad that I need to look for another job right now?"

Diana was looking through some papers. "Well, there's good news and bad news."

"OK," said Zaf. "Hit me with the good."

"The good is that I'm slowly getting a grip on how Paul was managing to keep costs down in recent months."

"Yes?"

"The bad was that he mostly managed that by reducing our spend on advertising and marketing."

Zaf tried to wrap his head round this. "So...?"

"We've been struggling to drum up business. With his

focus on that Londiniumarium travesty, we weren't making the bookings we might have. So, with income down, he decided to slash our advertising budget."

"Which meant even fewer people were making bookings," said Newton.

"Exactly. Vicious circle."

"I'm sure there was meant to be some genuine good news," said Zaf.

"There is," said Diana. "Sort of. Our potential customers are still out there. From what I can see here, if we got a massive injection of cash then we could do a marketing blitz and fill up our tours."

"If we got a massive injection of cash," said Newton.

"Yes. Quite."

"That man." Zaf blew out an exasperated breath.

"That man is dead," Diana reminded him.

Zaf huffed and dunked his biscuit in his tea. "I never asked. Did he have family?"

"He never talked about them," said Diana. "There'll be a funeral at some point. We, as respectful colleagues, will attend. The police might take a while to release his body though, if this is being treated as murder."

Newton pulled at the edge of a printed sheet halfway down the pile. It looked like an old Wild West 'Wanted' poster.

"What's this?"

The poster had the words 'Have you seen this dog?' printed above what looked like an internet image of a Pomeranian pooch. 'Answers to the name of "Marengo". Important witness in a legal case. Reward available.'

"Have you been putting up wanted posters?" said Zaf.

Diana nodded, not guiltily but wearily. "From Belgravia,

through Hyde Park and up to Paddington. Someone *must* have seen this dog."

"I'm sorry?" said Newton. "What crime is this dog supposed to have witnessed?"

"This is all about Morris Walker's alibi," said Zaf.

Zaf had never met the former manager of the Chartwell and Crouch depot. He'd been sent to prison long before Zaf had come down to London.

Several years earlier, a website touting tickets for non-existent London tours and shows had taken hundreds of thousands of pounds, possibly millions, from perfectly ordinary customers. The website had presented itself as belonging to Chartwell and Crouch, but was no such thing. The tours didn't exist, the customers lost their money, and the resulting investigation brought the police straight to the door of Chartwell and Crouch and the office of one Morris Walker, pop musician turned tour company manager.

"It's to do with his alibi for when the fraudulently-taken money was withdrawn from the Hackney Mutual Bank," said Diana.

"I remember," said Newton. "He said he was at this café around the corner from, er, where was it?"

"The Best Western Hotel in Sussex Gardens," replied Diana. "Said he'd gone there to write songs. He could even recount what he'd ordered – a mushroom and ham bruschetta – and mentioned little details like an older woman in a hat."

"With a little Pomeranian dog called Marengo," said Zaf.

"But the courts proved that the café didn't exist," said Newton.

"At least, there was no café that matched his description," said Diana. "The only shop around the corner from that hotel was a greasy spoon, and no one there recalled seeing him."

"Surely the bank had CCTV inside," said Newton.

"No. It's one of those weird little London banks. Only one branch, and that without any security cameras at all."

"Sounds dodgy," said Newton.

"Possibly is," Diana agreed. "Or at least, it's the kind of financial institution that appeals to unsavoury characters with dodgy dealings."

Newton shook his head. "But you're still looking for this imaginary dog who can back up Morris's alibi."

"I've seen him," said Zaf. "Or at least, I saw a Pomeranian dog and a woman owner calling it 'Marengo'. I was doing my final assessment for my Guild of Tourism certificate the other month and I saw the woman and heard the name on the Kings Road just down from Sloane Square."

"So you see," said Diana. "There is yet hope of exonerating Morris Walker."

"Funny, that. We were just talking about him."

They looked up to see Detective Chief Inspector Sugarbrook, standing in the doorway of the kitchen.

He pointed behind him. "We knocked at the outer door but no one answered."

"You are aware that you have a very noisy cat locked up in that little office?" added Detective Sergeant Quigley.

"Boudicca is going to become a music star, along with Gus here," Newton told her, puffing out his chest.

"Is that so?" said Sugarbrook. "I'd love to hear more but I'm afraid I need to ask you three some questions."

"We gave our statements at the studio on Abbey Road," said Zaf.

"Yes," agreed Sugarbrook. "But it has come to light that some employees of Chartwell and Crouch might have had reason to wish Paul Kensington dead."

Chapter Twenty-One

Diana stared at the detective. "Do you care to be more specific?"

DCI Sugarbrook raised an eyebrow. "Not just yet, no."

Zaf walked over to the closed door of Paul's office. Diana could see his hands trembling. He leaned against the door-frame and sniffed. "Boudicca's not going to like it in there."

"Has anyone been in there since he died?" asked Sugarbrook.

"All of us," said Diana. "Me in particular."

She caught the look in the DCI's eye. For a man with a face like a granite monument, Sugarbrook had tellingly expressive eyes.

"There's still a business to run here," she said. "What remains of the business, anyway."

"Yes." Sugarbrook dropped the word heavily.

"We need to get Boudicca over to the recording studio anyway," said Zaf. "So, let's talk logistics."

"How do you plan to transport Boudicca?" asked Diana.

"She can be a handful," said Newton. "But I've got a dog carrier case out back."

"How will that help?" asked Zaf. "She'll just have more room to take a run up."

"Because we can put her in the cat carrier and then put the cat carrier inside the dog carrier. It's like belt and braces, yeah?"

It was an odd but effective idea, Diana thought.

"We going by taxi, yeah?" said Zaf. "We'll never carry them both otherwise. So you're going to put Boudicca in the cat carrier?"

Zaf really didn't want to be the one who went into Paul Kensington's office and tried to put Boudicca into a carrier.

"We did it before and we can do it again," said Newton.

Zaf didn't much like the 'we' part of that.

The detectives were content to stand by and watch while Zaf and Newton teamed up to capture Boudicca. The vicious cat was wary of the sardines this time, and tried to seize one with a violent running jump, but somehow Newton caught her as she scrambled away, and swept her into the carrier. He dabbed antiseptic onto his scratched arms as Zaf secured her inside her double-walled prison.

"Is she Hannibal Lecter or something?" said Quigley.

"You clearly don't know this cat," Newton replied.

Sugarbrook had asked some questions of Zaf and Newton while they waited for their taxi. It was only a few minutes, but he had no power to hold them.

Once Zaf and Newton had set out with the two future music stars, Diana and Sugarbrook sat in the kitchen with a fresh pot of tea.

"You've known Paul Kensington for a long time," said Sugarbrook.

"I couldn't give it in months and weeks," she told him, "but yes."

"And how would you describe him as a person?"

Diana found herself smiling.

"Something funny?" asked Sugarbrook.

"You ask me to describe him *as a person*. It implies that he could be described as something other than a person."

"I've already gathered the impression that he was not especially... personable."

"No." She wrapped her fingers around the mug in front of her. The warmth of the drink through the pottery was pleasant. "You're an intelligent man, detective. Do you know what a eulogy is, I mean, where the word comes from?"

He lifted his eyes to think for a second. "'Eu' means good. Eulogy. To speak good words of the dead."

"I honestly don't know why we do that," Diana said. "Yes, out of kindness to the nearest, to the bereaved. But if we're being honest, we should speak truthfully about the dead. Diana Bakewell was an interfering busybody with a thousand friends but no one who really loved her."

"That's not true, I'm sure."

"We will see," she said. "I could speak in half-lies about Paul Kensington but..."

"But?"

She took a few seconds to compose her thoughts.

"Paul was not a bad human being. He was infuriating and selfish and petty. He was a short-sighted, unimaginative and financially incapable manager. He was all of these things not because he was a bad man but because he was a useless one.

He was..." She tightened her lips. "Forgive me, but he was a ten year-old boy who had been dropped into the body of a man. I wonder if he spent his entire adult life with the fear that people would realise he was a complete incompetent. Maybe he didn't realise that we already viewed him that way."

"You don't mince your words, Miss Bakewell."

"But he was not a bad person."

"I wonder what attributes you think would make someone a bad person."

She looked at him levelly. "Someone who would push Paul Kensington off a fire escape stair, deliberately or accidentally, and then run off rather than stop and help."

"You didn't like him."

"I try hard to find something to like in everyone," she said. "If you live in London, you will meet the full spectrum of humanity. There's no point wasting your energy on hatred."

"But you're glad he's no longer manager of Chartwell and Crouch."

She frowned. "Is that what this is about? You think one of us would kill him to get rid of a useless boss? Goodness, imagine if everyone with an awful manager decided to push them off a rooftop. You'd have corpses everywhere."

Sugarbrook took out a notepad but did not open it.

"At the launch event on Friday, one of your colleagues was heard saying that you would make an infinitely better boss than Paul."

She thought about Detective Sergeant Quigley poking around Paul's office. What would she find there?

"Would you?" said Sugarbrook.

"To be frank, the cat that's been squatting in that office this afternoon would make a better manager than Paul was. This is not a motive for murder."

"'The sooner he dies, the better.'"

"Pardon?"

He flipped open his notepad. "Newton Crombie uttered those words at the launch party, according to a witness."

"People are permitted to speak figuratively and vent their feelings, especially when there's complimentary alcohol on offer."

"People do other things under the influence of alcohol too," Sugarbrook pointed out.

Diana pressed her lips together and made an annoyed grunt.

"Paul's thoughtlessness was stripping away our jobs and any joy we had in them. Newton has driven and tended to our vintage buses for years, and now all but one of them has been sold off. I shouldn't be surprised if that one's gone before long."

"I've irritated you," Sugarbrook said.

"You have!" she snapped back.

"How? You don't anger easily. You've even just said so."

"How? How?" Diana picked up her tea, then realised she was too annoyed to drink it and put it down with an unnecessary clatter. "Let me list the reasons. Newton is the most ridiculously sweet human being you could ever meet. He once invited more than twenty cats into our depot because he couldn't stand to see them go hungry. Yes, he is angry about the loss of the buses and, soon enough, his job. But he is no murderer."

"People surprise us when—"

"But more than that," she continued hotly, "Paul is dead and my old friend Pascal Palmer is laid up in hospital with a head injury that I – well, no one is telling me what's going on there. At our age, it only takes one thing to tip us over the edge. He could be dying right now for all I know."

"I believe he's in a stable condition but, as you say, at *his* age they want to keep a good eye on him."

"While you're busy following all the wrong leads," said Diana.

"Oh?" Sugarbrook smiled. She was simmering with anger and he was amused. "Really? Please tell me what I should be doing."

She eyed him. "The attacker confronted Pascal first. If you're looking for cause, if you're looking for motive, then you would do well to consider who might have reason to hurt Pascal."

Sugarbrook looked at his notepad again.

"'Ariadne and Pascal can't bear each other even now.'" He looked at her. "You said that. At the launch."

"Someone was listening very closely, weren't they?" she said, knowing it sounded bitter.

"Ariadne Webb couldn't account for her actions in that vital minute before you heard Pascal being attacked. She said she was going downstairs to get a fresh glass of fizz but no one else can honestly confirm that."

"She went into Studio Three in a mask –?"

"She knew Pascal was there," said Sugarbrook.

" – in a mask, and made demands of him in a gruff voice?"

"You said it was a middling voice. Man or woman."

"I think if Ariadne wanted to kill Pascal, she wouldn't have waited a lifetime to do so."

"Oh," said Sugarbrook with a thoughtful tilt of his block-like head, "sometimes people wait until their golden years before deciding to deal with unfinished business."

The door opened and Quigley entered, a key in her hand.

"Do you know what this is?" Quigley asked Diana.

Diana had seen it before. "It's a locker key, isn't it? For

somewhere nearby. Paul didn't know why it was in his office, if that helps."

"We should check it out," said Sugarbrook.

"Really?" said Diana.

He nodded. "I have a theory about this crime, and I would love to get your reaction to it. Come on. Let's go take a look."

Chapter Twenty-Two

Zaf was nervous about the sound test, but he was trying hard not to show it. He was nervous that Newton was so far down the rabbit hole of trying to train the two cats to sing, he might never come back out. Most of all, though, he was nervous about crossing London with the two cats, one of which was hell-bent on escaping and killing things, not necessarily in that order.

The two cats could not have been more different. Boudicca caught sight of Gus on the short drive over to St John's Wood and hissed at him. Gus simply settled into a relaxed position to observe her better, as if she was the cat equivalent of a character in a soap opera.

They unloaded at the recording studio on Abbey Road and Ken Ferrari came out to meet them with a sling over his arm and shoulder.

"Hello, hello! Let me help you with the boxes," he said, although he was of course in no physical state to help them. The help came from a young runner in a T-shirt printed with the Fab Four from the Yellow Submarine movie.

"The stars of our show need to be treated right, eh?" said Ken. "I know star quality when I see it."

They went inside. Newton took Ken to one side, and gave him a serious look.

"You need to know what you're dealing with here. Boudicca may not look dangerous, but she is as cunning as she is powerful. Do not allow yourself to be alone in a room with her. If she tries to persuade you to release her from her restraints then you must not listen."

Ken laughed. "I've dealt with them all. Music people are wonderful human beings, for the most part. The occasional diva. I'm a producer. If there's musical gold to be squeezed out of these darlings then I will do it."

"But you need to be careful," said Newton earnestly.

Half an hour later they had released Gus into the cavernous Studio One and let Boudicca out in one of the sound booths, where the door was carefully locked. Boudicca stalked around, angrily raking her claws across a stool here and a carpet square there.

"So today we'll practise getting sounds from the two of them and come up with a plan for the actual recording day," said Ken. "Today is prep, then we do recordings and then you lot all get to go home while me and my mixing genius, Tracy, work it all together. Shall we work with Gus first, give the feisty one a chance to settle in?"

It sounded good in practice, but Zaf wasn't convinced that Boudicca would become any more compliant. Gus behaved impeccably, voicing his own range of sounds.

"He's a bloomin' good puss, that one," said Chaz Chase, watching from the doorway with a clipboard in his hand.

"A pleasure to work with," said Ken. "I think we're gonna get some nice little parts from him."

Newton glowed with paternal pride.

"Shall we have a go with dear Boudicca, then?" said Ken,

Newton explained that they had managed to get Boudicca to respond to the screeching sounds from the underground. He got out his phone to demonstrate.

"Good, good. Let's give it a try then, shall we?"

Ken had the means to play sounds into the studio where Boudicca was confined, and they all watched carefully while he played the sounds of the tube. Boudicca, hackles raised, located the speaker that was making the noise and gave it a savage bite, worrying a piece of plastic away from the edge.

"Blimey, she's a tricksy one, ain't she?" said Chaz.

"Let's give her a minute," said Ken, completely chilled.

They gave her half an hour, but Boudicca refused to comply. She continued her rampage round the studio, attacking inanimate objects at random.

"Let's take a break for lunch, shall we?" said Chaz. "Ken, can you sign off on these expenses?"

Ken took the clipboard and, as Chaz left, leaned aside to Zaf. "You can tell someone who hasn't spent their career in the music business," he whispered. "Normal people expect to get their lunch breaks, their two tea breaks a day. Music people, true music people, have been trained to go for days without sustenance."

"Chaz seems enthusiastic, though," said Zaf.

Ken jiggled his head in a charitable sort of gesture. "Most people who decide to buy their way into the music business, they're of a type."

"Oh?"

"Usually it's a mid-life crisis. Some businessman who's hit the age of fifty and thought, 'blow me, I've not done anything fun with my life' and decides to set up a recording studio. A lot of wealthy divorcees try to get in on this business. They're parted from their cash soon enough. They go out looking for talent and see some skinny teenager leaping about on stage in a leopard-skin top and they think they're seeing raw talent like they're witnessing the second coming."

"But it's not."

Ken shook his head. "What they're seeing, what they're entranced by, is a vision of youthful freedom, the thing this middle-aged investor has lost. But that's it, they're ensnared. And before long, this business has separated them from the contents of their bank account. Believe you me. Look at this."

On the clipboard was a series of expenditures under the Lamé Records business name. Food, furniture, equipment, vaguely defined services. The bill came to tens of thousands.

"Chaz is spending a fortune on this venture," said Zaf.

"Told you," said Ken.

"But Chaz isn't a wealthy divorcee."

"Nah, he's an honest and stand-up bloke."

Zaf could have spluttered with laughter. He'd met Chaz before many times and the man was many things – loyal, protective, funny, friendly – but he was not an honest and stand-up bloke. He was a career crook.

Chaz had snacks brought in from the *Let it Bean* café. Zaf grabbed a sandwich. He found Newton fretting over by the glass window of the studio.

"Hey, mate! It's not your fault she's being difficult."

Newton sighed. "I just hoped she might perform. I feel that she has some real star quality, you know?"

"Yeah," said Zaf, although he wasn't convinced. "It's as if she reacts to the tube trains because she's angry with them. Maybe we're just sort of annoying her."

Newton looked exasperated. "Have you ever seen her when she's not annoyed?"

"Well, no. I guess not. Maybe this is just her natural state."

Chapter Twenty-Three

Diana walked with DCI Sugarbrook and DS Quigley up Chiltern Street towards Marylebone Road and Baker Street station. Quigley held the locker key purposefully in her hand.

"You see, there's one thing really bothering me about this incident," said Sugarbrook, taking long slow strides to Diana's quick footsteps.

"I should imagine it's all quite... bothersome," she said.

"It's the money in Paul's pocket."

Diana frowned. "The fifty pound notes."

"Two out-of-circulation fifty pound notes."

"That's relevant?"

He gestured with a hand. "I'm not given to flights of wild speculation, but it made me think of someone else: the person who was not at that party."

"Who was *not* at the party?"

He nodded. "You were there. Pascal Palmer, Ariadne Webb and Ken Ferrari were there. Former members of Electra-Beat. Also Newton, Zaf and Paul Kensington, all employees of

Chartwell and Crouch. Chaz Chase was there along with Ernie Holland. Imagine a Venn diagram of those three groups, and there's one person who should have been there. If circumstances hadn't prevented it."

"Morris Walker."

He nodded. "Bingo. And what do we know about Morris Walker's crime?"

Diana eyed the DCI. "I don't believe he did it."

He scowled at her. "What we know is that, all those years ago, he withdrew the proceeds of his crime from that two-bit bank. He took the cash, and that money was never seen again."

"The out-of-circulation bank notes."

"Now mysteriously on Paul Kensington's person. So... what if it's possible? A gathering of people, all with some connection to Morris Walker. A man turns up dead, with what is potentially some of Morris's loot in his pocket. That's a motive to kill Paul right there, particularly if the killer knows more about Morris's crime than they've let on."

Diana thought it through as they waited for the lights to change so they could cross the busy road to Baker Street station.

"So," she said, "Paul has been in league with the thief all these years, and had access to the stolen money?"

"Possibly."

"But there's the attack on Pascal."

"The attacker said, 'Give it to me.' A reference to the money?"

"But in the unlikely event that this theory is remotely true, it was Paul who had the money, not Pascal."

"Hmmm." Sugarbrook frowned and fell silent.

"You started out this investigation thinking that the attack was made by an outsider. I hear you arrested Maxwell Best."

"A number of people are helping us with our enquiries."

Helping us with our enquiries. Diana scoffed. "But what if it *is* an outsider? Assuming this is even about the missing money, what if this outsider came looking for cash or answers or something, and they knew the person they wanted would be there? But what if they didn't know what the person they were after actually looked like?"

"Go on."

Diana mused on it. "Someone knows the person they seek is at that event. They come in. They look for them. The names 'Paul' and 'Pascal' are similar, if overheard. What if someone misidentified Pascal as the person they were interested in?"

"This is a bit of a leap of imagination."

"You're the one whose theory has Pascal getting attacked by someone after Paul's money," she countered. "What if the person was genuinely seeking Paul – though I really don't see that he has any proper link to the missing funds – and latched onto Pascal by mistake?"

Sugarbrook grunted. The lights changed, the green man flashed and they crossed.

Baker Street Luggage Drop was a short distance along Baker Street itself. It was a dour-looking business, the wide window mired with grime. Sugarbrook led the way inside and spoke to the young man at the counter, whose English was barely functional. But he led them through to the back.

The luggage drop business occupied one of those many London buildings that was very narrow at the front but seemed to extend backwards for unfathomably long distance, Doctor Who's Tardis, executed in good old brick and mortar. Out back there were banks and banks of old fashioned lockers. It looked like this business had emptied a leisure centre changing room during a refurbishment, and put the lockers to use here.

Quigley looked at the keyfob in her hand and counted off locker doors.

"We may be about to make a great discovery," said Sugarbrook with unaccustomed energy.

"This one." Quigley stopped before a large, ground-level locker.

"Please," said Sugarbrook, smiling now. "Do the honours."

Quigley crouched and put the key in the lock. It was stiff and did not turn at first. At last, with a metallic scrape, Quigley pulled it open.

Diana looked inside. Sugarbrook looked inside.

The locker was empty.

Chapter Twenty-Four

During lunch, Ken was deeply engaged in technical discussions with Tracy Chen about how best to record the cat vocals. Tracy repeatedly made it clear that cats couldn't be trusted to stay still long enough to record anything. While this discussion rumbled on, Chaz entered Studio One with Ariadne Webb.

Ken smiled. "Someone blessed with true star quality has dropped in to offer her advice."

Ariadne, dressed in a light summer dress and carrying an unmarked plastic bag, gave an airy wave to the group. "I've just come back from seeing dear Pascal in hospital, and I thought I'd see how everyone else is holding up."

Dear Pascal? thought Zaf. As far as he knew, Ariadne had nothing but spite for her ex.

"Well, this is a surprise," he said.

She turned her smile on him, then let it drop. "You and your little tour guide company must be reeling from what's happened."

"Something like that," muttered Newton.

Ariadne went to Ken and hugged him, careful to avoid his damaged shoulder. "We need to look after each other and look out for each other now, don't we?"

"Life is all a karmic circle," said Ken. "The love we take equal to the love we make and all that."

"Well, indeed," she replied. "Though I can't think what Pascal did to deserve that battering."

Was there a barbed note to her words?

"It's good you were able to get in to see Pascal," Zaf said. "Diana's been trying, but they told her it was immediate family only."

Ariadne gave a shrug. "Maybe it's that he's shown some progress. He's fully awake and aware now. Maybe it's because I lied and told them I was his sister. Now, what's going on here?"

While Ken explained the intricacies of recording an album of music by cats and for cats, Zaf sent a message to Diana, telling her that visiting Pascal might be an option.

"It's possible I can help with your cat problem," said Ariadne.

Newton looked suspicious. "Do you know much about cats?"

"Cats?" Ariadne laughed. "My mum has helped out at a cat rescue for years. I have known many, many cats. Now, where is this problem child of yours?"

"Boudicca's in there." Newton pointed to the booth. "But you can't go in. She's dangerous."

Ariadne gave him a look of supreme confidence. "I can go in, and I will."

She stepped over to the studio door, opened it, let herself in, and closed the door. Zaf, Newton, Ken and Chaz all pressed up against the glass to watch.

"Get ready with the antiseptic and the plasters," said Newton.

Ariadne approached Boudicca, sitting regally in the shredded chair and staring at the intruder. She swept the cat up into her arms. Boudicca struggled for a moment, but Ariadne had the cat clamped firmly in her embrace. There was some wriggling, but after a few seconds Boudicca relented.

"She must have scratches all down her arms," whispered Newton. "I'm pretty sure I've tried what she just did."

Ariadne sat down on the chair and stroked Boudicca, tickling her behind the ears. She reached into the plastic bag and pulled out a piece of meat. It looked orange and slimy. Boudicca took it in her mouth, sat a small distance away and chewed with a contented expression.

"What is that?" breathed Newton. "Has she given Boudicca some sort of drug?"

"Niiiice," sang Ariadne in a quiet but tuneful voice. "Niiice."

There was a brief chirp of approval from Boudicca. It wasn't singing, but it was definitely a sound.

"Oi oi! Looks like she might just be onto summat!" said Chaz.

"Positive reinforcement," said Newton. "What is that stuff she's feeding to her?"

"Looks like fish to me," said Chaz.

"Huh." Newton turned to Zaf, who shrugged back at him.

"This will give us what we need for the sound check," said Ken. "Mission accomplished. It's a good job Chaz has given us unlimited time and expenditure for this project."

Afterwards, when the required recording had been made, Ariadne came out, carefully closing the door behind her.

"That was magical," said Zaf.

"Salmon from the kosher deli on Circus Road never fails to please," she said. "Sadly, that was supposed to be my lunch."

"I think we can probably treat you to something at Chaz's café," said Newton.

"A bite to eat would be lovely."

Chapter Twenty-Five

Leaving Ken and Tracy to work on the recordings and Boudicca to rest from her singing session, Zaf and Newton took Ariadne to the *Let it Bean* café attached to the studio.

"Let's see what puns are on the menu today," said Ariadne. "Pascal has firm opinions on joke titles for food."

They found a free table by the window. Ariadne eyed the menu critically and ordered the Octopus's Garden Salad. Zaf and Newton had already had lunch, but Newton ordered a Magical Mystery Torte. There were mugs of tea to start, into which Ariadne heaped spoonsful of sugar. Gus sat in his carrier under the table and washed himself.

"You handled Boudicca without getting a single mark on you," Newton marvelled.

"I seem to have spent my life handling prickly customers." Ariadne sipped her tea, then added another spoon of sugar. "How is Diana holding up, by the way?"

"She's helping the police with their inquiries," said Newton.

Zaf tutted at his colleague. "The police wanted to have a look round Paul's office at work. Diana is busting a gut just trying keep the depot ticking over."

"She will make a brave effort," said Ariadne, "but I do think you gentlemen should dust off your CVs. I can even put a good word in for you with Tom. ACE Tours is a fine employer."

"What kind of buses do you have?" asked Newton. "You have some of those Urbis two-point-five DD Open Tops, don't you?"

"What Newton means," said Zaf, interjecting, "is that it's a kind offer, but we need to think about what's best for all of us, collectively. That includes Diana."

Ariadne gave Zaf a penetrating look, just as the waiter returned with the food order. Newton's torte might have been magical, but it didn't seem very mysterious. It was a lemon torte, plain and simple. Ariadne picked up her knife and fork to tackle her salad.

"I am sure ACE Tours could find a place even for someone like Diana," she said.

"You two? Under the same roof?" Zaf tried to keep his tone light.

"We were once the very best of friends. Inseparable."

"Well, what on earth happened?" asked Newton, jabbing his fork into his torte.

Ariadne sat back and took a deep breath. "We grew up together, and in our teens, we were seized with this mad notion of making it big in the music industry. We thought we could do it by hanging out with all the cool music people. We went to all the parties and chatted to all the right people." She laughed. "And all the *wrong* people. We could so easily have been chewed up and spat out."

She prodded her food but didn't take a bite.

"I'm sure Diana has told you we rented a flat together from George Harrison. The coolest and most handsome of the Fab Four, and an astonishing guitarist."

"Together?" said Newton.

Ariadne looked at Zaf. "That Eccleston Square flat you've been enjoying until recently was the place we rented off George. He let the whole place out to musical types. Zaf, don't think I didn't recognise that lime green suit as one of Bryan's. It was while we were staying there that we met Morris and Pascal. They'd already formed ElectraBeat and put out their first album. It didn't do well. But they had the idea that adding in some female vocalists might provide the necessary magic and – well – clearly we did."

"That's when you recorded *Count Me In*," said Zaf.

Ariadne nodded. "Number three in the charts. And in those days, the beginning of the eighties, records could spend weeks and weeks in the charts. Yeah, we made it big. And we were younger then than you are now, Zaf. Fame and fortune can come too soon, you know."

"It must have been amazing, though."

Ariadne smiled. "It was. It was amazing. But we made mistakes along the way. My biggest was probably falling in love with Pascal Palmer. He was a few years older than me and so, so very good looking back then. I moved out of the flat, sub-let it to Diana, and moved in with him. Possibly the most terrible decision of my life, although it didn't feel like that for many years."

She finally put a fork piled with shredded leaves and sliced tomatoes into her mouth and ate.

"It all comes crashing down eventually," she said. "George, not that long before he died, sold off that house in Eccleston Square to that Dadashov guy."

"Kamran Dadashov," Zaf muttered.

A shrug. "Morris had invested wisely, and used his money to buy into Chartwell and Crouch. He got Diana a job with them too. I was still handcuffed to that self-destructive alcoholic, Pascal. Didn't matter that he was getting himself cleaned up, the damage was done. I got a job as a tour guide, but with ACE Tours, obviously."

"You and Diana are so alike."

Ariadne chuckled. "In many, many ways. But when ElectraBeat imploded, and that band truly imploded, we all ended up picking sides. And it took me several years to realise that, when the battle lines were drawn, it was those three on one side and me on the other. Me, alone in the cold."

"I'm sorry to hear that," said Zaf.

"When Morris and Pascal fell out, Diana sided with the man who'd kept hold of his money, not the one who'd drunk his fortune away. And when Pascal and I parted ways, after I sacrificed so much of my life trying to fix him, to heal him, Diana presented herself as a shoulder for him to cry on. She always made the astute move."

The sigh that came out of her mouth was sharp. Pained even.

"Never underestimate Diana's ability to do what suits her best." She stabbed at her salad. "When Pascal was attacked the other day, were either of you with Diana?"

"I was," said Zaf.

She must have caught a flicker of an expression on his face because she raised an eyebrow.

"I was initially," said Zaf, "but then I went downstairs to find another way up to the second floor."

"So, you weren't *actually* with her," said Ariadne.

"You don't think she could have possibly attacked Pascal and Paul?" said Newton.

Ariadne shrugged as though bored of the notion now. "If you do want to think about who might have wanted to hurt Pascal, you ought to take a look at this."

She opened her small handbag and pulled out a piece of folded paper.

"I still keep some newspaper clippings," she said as she unfolded it. "Don't ask me why but I do. But that—" She flicked the paper. "That is motive right there."

Zaf looked at the article that had been cut carefully out of a London paper.

"Flaming heck," whispered Newton. "That *is* a motive."

Chapter Twenty-Six

Diana found herself fussing around the Chartwell and Crouch depot on Wednesday morning, a new habit she'd picked up since she'd been evicted from the apartment in Eccleston Square. When she'd lived in the sub-divided house in Eccleston Square, that sorting and straightening behaviour had often been devoted to tidying her own flat and then going out and neatening up the front gardens of some of the unoccupied houses in the square, of which there were many. Pots were watered, weeds were plucked and bits of rubbish were put in bins.

Only now could she see that this behaviour had been as much about preparing for the day as it had been community-minded good deed. Now, sharing a less-than-spacious flat with her mum, there was little for her to do first thing except maybe a little washing up and therefore, with tidying energy still to burn, she had started 'fussing' at the depot once she'd got to work.

Cat bowls were cleaned, health and safety posters on the walls were straightened and any remaining brochures were rearranged or gathered to take out to hand to passersby in the tourist hotspots. As soon as Zaf and Newton arrived, she found herself issuing instructions and information, as though she had been their manager for years.

The email she'd received from Chartwell and Crouch's parent company, TripTastic, had given her cause for concern. A woman named Rita de la Cruz was coming to "check in" with them and make sure everyone was OK. But reading between the lines, Diana knew the visit would be an audit of the Chiltern Street depot as an ongoing business.

She wanted to be ready to answer any questions the woman might ask. She might not agree with some of Paul Kensington's decisions, but she at least needed to understand what they were. And she needed the depot to look professional.

"I'm going to visit Pascal in hospital today," she told her colleagues, "but we've got the woman from head office coming in tomorrow, so I would like this place to be spick and span."

"Gus and Boudicca have another recording session at Abbey Road today," said Newton.

"I can see how that's important, but we also want to present the best versions of ourselves for the head office woman. Please, let's just look busy."

"We'll do what's needed to save our jobs."

Diana felt her shoulders slump. "Listen. Newton, Zaf. I think we need to face up to the possibility it's curtains for Chartwell and Crouch."

Newton folded his arms across his chest. "Never say never."

"I'm just saying we need to be realistic. It's time we all started to think about where we might find another place to work."

"Right," said Zaf. "I see." He sounded like he really didn't.

"So what we need to find," said Newton, "is a place that needs two tour guides and a driver mechanic. Anyone got any leads?"

Zaf and Diana looked at him. Diana realised that Newton was going to have the most trouble processing this.

"Mate," said Zaf, "you do know your skills are much more transferable than that, don't you?"

Newton looked at him blankly. "No? I'm not sure I do know that. I need someone to tell me what to do, and if it's not you two, then who is it?"

Diana sighed. Newton was clever – he knew those buses inside and out. But he wasn't getting the message.

"There must be a ton of jobs that need your mechanical knowhow," Zaf said. "Anybody who has, er, mechanical things would jump at the chance to have you, wouldn't they?"

Diana seized the challenge. "Zaf's right, Newton. You might think this was your ideal job, but I bet if you dared to dream really big, there's something out there you'd really love to do. What's the most fun vehicle or machine that you could picture yourself working on?"

"I see what you're trying to do," said Newton, "and it's kind of you, but I'm not sure – oh! The mechanism that raises the bascules for Tower Bridge! Imagine working on something like that. Vintage, completely bespoke and absolutely massive."

"That's the spirit!" Diana found herself smiling. "Now, why don't you spend a few minutes making a list of the dream things you'd like to work on. Get as many things on there as you can and then we can do some searches, see what we can find."

Newton pulled a notebook from the pocket of his overall and started to write.

Diana looked at Zaf. "How about you Zaf? Do you have any immediate thoughts?"

"Apart from blind panic?" Zaf shrugged. "I can just go back to Birmingham if I run out of options. I do love it here, though. Every time I thought I'd run out of options before, something turned up. Now I really can't see where the next break might come from."

"Zaf. Are you forgetting that you are now certified by the Guild of Tourism? You're a hot property, and there are definitely opportunities out there for you. You seemed to be getting on well with Tom Griffin the other day. Have you asked him if he has any vacancies?"

Zaf looked wary. "I mean, he seemed nice, but it would be sort of wrong, surely?"

Diana made a show of rolling her eyes. "Wrong? No! Don't even think about telling yourself that it would be disloyal to me or something like that. ACE Tours is an amazing company and Tom Griffin is a great boss. Yes, I have some history with Ariadne, but that shouldn't affect you. Please make it your business to get hold of Tom and let him know you're interested in working for him."

"I will," said Zaf. "And you're definitely fine with that?"

"I am definitely fine with that."

She looked at him, still smiling, but there was a worry behind that smile. Should she have been so enthusiastic, what with one ACE Tours employee *and* the owner still on her mental list of people who might have killed Paul?

Chapter Twenty-Seven

"Looms!" yelled Newton, clapping his hands.

Diana and Zaf both jumped.

"Sorry, what?" said Zaf.

Newton was on his phone, waving it around. "I was searching for places with vacancies, using some keywords I thought might flush out anyone using cool vintage machinery. Well, I found one! An artisanal weaver over in Shoreditch. Can you imagine how much fun it would be to work on some of that fine machinery from the old textile mills?"

"Did they have textile mills in Shoreditch?" asked Zaf. He pictured textile mills as being a Northern thing.

"Dunno," said Newton. "Looms are great. I saw one once in Wales that was completely water powered. Had a drive shaft connected with the river outside."

Diana nodded. "Spitalfields was famous for weaving when it was filled with Huguenot refugees back in the seventeenth and eighteenth centuries. It's great that you've found something to apply for so quickly. What's your next move?"

"I've already applied for the job." Newton sat back in his chair, looking triumphant.

Zaf started to speak, then closed his mouth. How had Newton applied for a job while they were all just sitting there? Every time Zaf had applied for a job it had taken hours and hours, crafting the perfect CV then fretting over the wording of the application letter. The places that used a portal to process job applications were even worse because you had to juggle the same information into different formats every time.

"That was speedy," said Diana. "How did you get an application together so quickly?"

"They said that I should send them an email saying why I'm the best person for the job, so I sent them that picture Zaf took of me."

Zaf frowned. "The one where you're in the inspection pit waving a spanner like a maniac?"

"That's the one."

"The one where you're smeared with so much engine oil that you look as if you could lubricate the bus just by rubbing your face on it?"

Newton scowled. "I thought it showed a keenness to get stuck in."

"I am certain that it did," said Diana. "And if you come across any other roles that you want to apply for, Newton, I am very happy to assist you with the process."

Zaf smiled at Diana.

"Well, I must be off," she said. "Busy day."

"Before you go see Pascal," said Zaf, "I have to show you this." He held out a folded newspaper clipping. "Ariadne gave it to me."

Diana unfolded it and read. It was a restaurant review.

During my ill-fated visit to Let it Bean, *an establishment that prides itself on a Beatles theme just as much as it does on culinary mediocrity, I had the misfortune of sampling what can only be described as a gastronomic tragedy. The Sgt. Pepper's Lonely Hearts Club Sandwich was as disheartening as its namesake was inspiring, a bland, overpriced assemblage of dry chicken and wilted lettuce, utterly lacking in the promised 'peppery' zing. The coup de grâce, however, was the Long and Winding Rocky Road. This dessert, far from the delightful treat one might anticipate, was a miserly portion of stale marshmallows and lacklustre chocolate, an utterly disappointing end to a meal. The ethos of this café, if one can indeed be discerned from its offerings, appears to be a dire attempt at capitalizing on Beatlemania with no genuine soul or flavourful harmony to be found.*

Diana looked at Zaf. "This is one of Pascal's reviews?"

"Of Chaz's café," he said.

"And you think...?"

Zaf shrugged.

She passed it back to him. "If restaurateurs attacked every critic who gave them a bad review..."

"Reviewers would be a lot nicer in future?"

"And Ariadne just happened to give that to you?" She twisted her lips together.

"It kind of came up naturally."

Diana wasn't buying it. "We'll talk about this later."

She headed for the door. She could get to the Royal Free Hospital by bus, but was planning to take the tube to Swiss Cottage and walk the mile from there. But as she made her way to Baker Street underground, her phone rang.

"Hello?" she said.

"What do you want with my mum's dog?" said a voice.

"I'm sorry?"

"You been putting up all these posters about my mum's dog?"

It took Diana a second to understand what the woman was on about.

"Marengo?" she said. "Your mum's dog is called Marengo?"

"It is."

"And it's a Pomeranian?"

"It is. And it's hers and she don't want to be involved in no legal nonsense!"

"There's no nonsense. There's a very serious matter that you or your mum might be able to help me with."

"We're not interested. My mum's not interested. I'm phoning to tell you to take your posters down."

"Please," said Diana, fearing the woman might hang up. "I'm literally just trying to find a café."

"A what?"

"Look, it's complicated. But basically a friend of mine is in prison because—"

"I don't want to get involved in no criminal stuff."

"Please, it's not that. My friend gave a statement about a café he visited where there was a woman matching your mum's description, but I can't find it or at least can't seem to match the café that's there with the one he described."

"What café?" said the woman.

"Just some pleasant little café near Sussex Gardens where your mum was—"

The woman tutted. "Savage Gardens."

"Sorry? What?"

"You mean Savage Gardens."

Diana knew Savage Gardens. It was a cut through street, not far from the Tower of London. Miles away from Sussex Gardens.

"Are you sure?" she said.

"It's where she meets her friend, Maggie. It's a straight hop along the District Line for her. They've been going there for years. Place called Pepys Kitchen. You know, after the diary bloke."

"I do. I do," said Diana. "Pepys Kitchen. Savage Gardens."

"Is that all you needed to know?"

"I think it is." The woman's number had come up on Diana's phone. If she needed any more information, she could always call back.

"We're done? You don't need my mum no more?"

"You've been a great help. Thank you."

"And the, er, poster mentioned a reward?"

Diana tensed. "Yes, indeed. I just need to check it all out but – oh, wow – if this is true it could set a wrongly convicted man free. Thank you."

Savage Gardens was barely a fifteen minute tube ride from Baker Street. Pascal could wait.

Chapter Twenty-Eight

The Circle Line took Diana to Tower Hill where she exited the underground station, turned away from the Tower of London and walked up the incline towards Pepys Street. Savage Gardens was a short and unassuming road with a fearsome name. It was named after the equally fearsomely-named Viscount Savage, but Diana couldn't remember more than that.

At the top of Savage Gardens, the road met Pepys Street. The junction bounded by high rise offices and hotels but, set back from the street, there was a two-storey building that was very clearly a café or restaurant with the words 'Pepys Kitchen' in flowing white script across the large glass frontage.

Diana felt her heart lift with relief at seeing it. She crossed Pepys Street and hurried towards the café. Like many of the buildings round here, it was mostly glass, but the café owners had softened its appearance with large potted plants, both inside and out.

She pushed open the door and stepped inside. Seats were

arranged in a row of snug wooden booths along one wall, and there were high stools in front of a bar at the window.

Diana went to the counter. A balding man with Mediterranean features was refilling the salad display.

"Hello, lady," he said in a bright voice, without looking up. "What can I get you, eh?"

"Do you happen to serve bruschetta?" she asked.

"Absolutely. What kind?"

"Ham and mushroom?"

"Coming right up! Anything else?"

"And do you..." Her mouth felt dry. "Do you know if a woman comes in here with a little Pomeranian dog?"

"Marengo!" he grinned, still not looking up from his salad work.

Diana heard a yip. A snowy-white terrier emerged from a little wooden crate to the side of the counter.

"No, you silly goose. He is not here now!" said the man.

The fluffy dog continued to look around expectantly.

The man finally looked up at Diana. "Marengo and Tintin here are best of friends."

"Oh, that's lovely." Diana bent to stroke the dog. It backed off suspiciously and sniffed her fingers.

"You got sausage or cheese on you?" asked the man.

"No."

"Then Tintin ain't interested." He set to preparing the bruschetta sandwich. "What you want with Marengo, anyway?"

"Ah, this is an odd one."

The man laughed. "We enjoy the odd ones. All of life comes in here. Mr Tom Cruise the other day. Ordered the giant meat platter. Enjoyed it so much he ordered the same entire dish again. True story."

"This one is much longer ago than that. Over seven years." Diana took out her phone. "This man came in. He ordered the ham and mushroom bruschetta and apparently had some sort of interaction with Marengo."

"OK. Do you want a drink with this?"

"A small coffee perhaps. I don't suppose you have any recollection of seeing him?"

"Seven years ago? Ha! Not likely. You don't know the exact date?"

"I don't. No, hang on, I do." She searched on her phone. It was Morris Walker's alibi for the time the money had been taken out of the bank, and the date had been mentioned in the press. "Yes. Yes. Here."

Her coffee was on the counter by the time she'd found what she was looking for. The café owner peered at the image and the date, then went to the laptop by the till.

"Don't tell me you have CCTV of that date?" she said.

He laughed. "No. I don't. I am café owner, not Big Brother. But..." He opened up a spreadsheet and began to scroll down. "What is this for? You looking for a runaway husband?"

"No. I'm – that's an interesting guess, by the way – I'm trying to overturn an unjust conviction."

"Ah, an innocent man, eh?" He continued scrolling. "Ham and mushroom bruschetta. Ah! Ah!"

"What is it?"

"It's the day we had the guitar duo in and – ah!"

"What? What is it?"

"Let me see again," he asked.

She held out her phone, and he peered at it intently.

"He is that man, no?"

"That man?"

"Yes. The..." He began to sing, quite badly. "*Count me in, pa-pa-pa, Count me in pa-pa-pa...*"

"Yes!" Diana exclaimed. "Morris was the lead singer of ElectraBeat. Yes! He was here!"

"Sure," the man replied with a wink. "I remember all the celebrities. He was here. That day. Ham and mushroom bruschetta."

"Oh, my goodness, that's fantastic!"

"Yes. Great song. I liked it very much. I remember that one of the backing singers in the video was sultry and beautiful."

"Oh? Really?" She wanted to stop herself asking but couldn't. "Which one?"

He shrugged. "The one..." He made a duck-face pout.

"Did she look like she was trying too hard?" she asked.

"I don't know. Couldn't say. Very hot. Does things to a young man."

"Well, thank you," she said, backing away from the conversation rapidly. "Can I have my bruschetta to go, please."

Chapter Twenty-Nine

Diana arrived at the Royal Free Hospital half an hour later, her whole body fizzing with happy energy. She burned to share the news with Pascal.

His ward was in the East Wing on the seventh floor. Despite the confounding layout that hospitals seemed to specialise in, she found him soon enough. Pascal sat in a comfortable armchair beside his bed, a light paisley dressing gown wrapped around his button-up pyjamas and a copy of the London Evening Standard open across his lap.

"Ah, a visitor!" he declared, folding the paper.

Diana bent to kiss his cheek. There was a light dressing on his head. It looked such a minor injury now.

"If I had known you were coming, I would have sent out for room service," he told her.

"I'm way ahead of you," she replied, holding up two paper bags. "I popped into Giacobazzi's across the road. Pastries and sandwiches."

He winked. "I do like Italian food."

He unpacked the bags with pleasure. "Mortadella,

provolone and sun-dried tomatoes. Lovely. Ah, the duck liver pate with chilli jelly and salad. This is very kind of you, Diana."

She pulled over another armchair. They were the functional armchairs found in institutions everywhere, but the seat was comfortable, and when a nurse stuck his head in to ask if either of them wanted a cup of tea, Diana felt they could not have asked for more.

"They've kept you in for nearly a week now," she said. "But you look well."

"Oh, it seems my body is a medical game of whack-a-mole," he replied. "Having given myself a fearsome whack on the head, everything else started playing up. They thought I had concussion at first."

"You were delirious when I found you."

"You called me your 'love', I remember that much," he said with a raffish smile.

"Delirious, as I said."

She took a corner of one of the sandwiches to nibble.

"And once they were happy I hadn't suffered any brain damage, my blood pressure and heart rate were... one was too high and the other too low, I forget which way round it was. And they've been poking and monitoring me every half hour since then. But I think they'll be able to let me know what's going on within the next day."

"You just need to rest up," she told him.

"Precisely," he said and took a large bite of the mortadella sandwich. "Give me a month and this will just be another chapter in my memoirs."

"Are you writing your memoirs?"

His look was cool and playful. "I've jotted a few things here and there. My agent – oh, yes, I have an agent – says my life story has a nice redemption arc. I think she wants a 'my battle with the bottle' kind of confessional, but I hope I can rustle up something more nuanced."

"And when did your 'battle' begin?"

He narrowed his eyes at her. "You know this better than almost anyone. When you were my secret wine-taster at the turn of the century, while I was pretending to the world that Pascal Palmer was sampling food and drink all over London. You quizzed me deeply about my alcoholism."

"Oh, that I did. You were clean by then and had been working on that for, well, most of the nineties. I suppose I'm wondering when do you think it *started*?"

"When did I start drinking? We were all drinking back then."

"I remember a lot of parties," she said. "And I'm sure there were plenty I don't remember."

"After being stuck in a studio for six weeks solid, never seeing the light of day, I think we all went a little mad when we came out into the sunlight."

Diana nodded. "It was intense. After recording *Taunt*, I think we partied for a straight week."

He adopted a wistful smile. "We visited Rome, Capri and Cairo, all in ten days. Helicopter, yacht, cocktails, cocktails, cocktails."

She laughed. "We were young idiots."

"Idiots definitely. Riding that buzz. I thought I could drum in a band and produce hit albums for the next thirty years." He licked a smidge of chilli jam off his finger and pointed at her. "You want my 'battle with the bottle'? It was before we even started recording the third album. Everyone talks about the difficult second album. It was the difficult third album for us. We used to drink because it was fun. But it was after *Taunt* when I knew – secretly knew – I was drinking to cope."

That sounded right. "Eighty-two," she said.

He looked to the window, the light picking out an expression of surprise on his face. "It would have been. And I didn't even start to get myself straight until at least eight years later. Bloody hell, Diana. I don't know how you lot put up with me."

"If I recall correctly, we didn't." She munched on her sandwich.

"Do you think you could forgive me?" he asked.

"Forgiven, forgotten. As I said to the police yesterday, I don't have the time or energy to cling onto hatred."

"Then you're a better person than me," said Pascal, then frowned. "The police?"

"They came to the depot. Investigating the attack on you and Paul Kensington."

"I thought they'd arrested someone."

"Hmm. Maxwell Best? I think that was an old-fashioned knee-jerk police reaction. Something happens, arrest the nearest bloke who looks a bit shifty."

"Oh. Oh, I see."

"So, you didn't recognise the person who attacked you?"

Pascal shook his head slowly.

"Man or woman?" she said.

"The police have asked me these questions."

"But surely you could tell."

He looked at her. She gazed back, feeling her heart rate pick up.

"It was a man," he said.

Chapter Thirty

Pascal's brow furrowed. "I was attacked by a man. At least, I think I was. I could only see his eyes but..." He folded the empty paper bag on his lap. "Those times we were deep into recording stuff in the studio. Like four weeks into recording an album and we were on the hundredth or two hundredth take of Ken's keyboard solo or we were doing vocals again and again and again. You remember that?"

Diana hadn't taken her gaze off his face. "I do."

"Sing *'in the symphony of us, love, count me in'* a hundred times over and the words lose all meaning."

Diana shuddered. She recalled exactly what he meant.

"Do it enough and revisit it enough and any initial truth is lost," said Pascal. "That's how that moment in the studio feels to me now. Did I see a man? Yes. Tell me it was a woman and I'll nod and go, 'yes, possibly'. All the questions and all the attempts to get details out of me, it circles and circles until it becomes a blur."

"I'm sorry." She reached out to pat his hand and he grasped her hand in his. His grip was dry and warm and tender.

"I want to put so much of this behind me."

"Hey, it's OK." She curled her hand into his.

"My memoir reads like a nightmare, you know that." He pulled in a breath. "What there is of it. A meteoric rock career shot down by addiction and in-fighting. A relationship with Ariadne that I destroyed piece by piece, as she stood by me all the while. I am one long cautionary tale, Diana."

She took in his deeply lined face, still handsome and lively after all these years.

"Ups and downs, Pascal. You sorted yourself out. You dried out. You made a living from writing, a truly respected food critic. Even now, you have the love and admiration of people around you."

"There's that word again: 'love'." There was a twinkle in his eye as he said it.

She smiled. "There are places to flirt with old friends, Pascal. May I suggest that your hospital bedroom is not one of them, regardless of how fetching your dressing gown might be."

He laughed and let go of her hand.

"Besides, we don't want to send your blood pressure up, or they'll never let you out." She patted his knee as she sat back. "But I'm not against making up for lost time."

He raised an eyebrow. She gave a genuine shrug. She had never sought a romantic relationship with Pascal. She had always liked him, but was that a strong enough base on which to build something new? At their age?

Maybe, at their age, it was absolutely enough.

"I should warn you," she said. "If you're expecting my life to be anything other than a train wreck then you are sorely mistaken. You are looking at a woman who's been kicked out of her home, is living with her eighty-something mum, is probably going to lose her job within the space of a month and who the police are keeping a close eye on because I might have wished my manager dead."

"Sounds like the complete package." He cocked his head. "Why are the police investigating the death of your manager, um, Paul, isn't it? I thought he was an innocent bystander."

"Hard to say. The police are now trying to draw a line between the money embezzled from Chartwell and Crouch and Paul's death."

"They think he had something to do with it?"

"They're looking for the money. He had a key to a locker near Baker Street. I genuinely think they expected to find the missing millions there."

"But they've already got their man, haven't they? Morris is several years into his sentence."

"Ah." She held up her finger. "*That* is my big news."

"Oh?"

"I think I've got the evidence to clear Morris's name."

"What?"

"Well, you know he said he was in a café at the time the money was being withdrawn from the bank?"

"The bank that conveniently has no CCTV. The café that is a complete figment of his imagination. I remember both well."

"But it's not. A figment, I mean. I tracked down the Pomeranian called Marengo. The café is near Savage Gardens, not Sussex Gardens. I don't know what happened there, but either Morris misremembered or the police wrote it down wrong or – I don't know which, but there *is* a café round the corner from the hotel in Savage Gardens."

"There's a café around every corner in London, Diana dear."

"Pepys Kitchen. A dear old woman with a Pomeranian

called Marengo frequents it. It serves the same bruschetta sandwiches Morris mentioned in his alibi."

"So, he knows a café. Big deal."

"And I showed the owner a photo of Morris and he thinks he remembers him."

Pascal was stunned for a moment, before finding his voice.

"*Thinks* he remembers him?"

"Oh, come on! This is great news. It's a vindication of everything Morris has been saying."

"It's certainly something. You've told the police about this?"

"Not yet." She sighed. "It feels tenuous. And I don't mean I doubt it. I want to solidify what this means. I need to talk to Morris first."

"You've not told him either?"

"Well, you can't just text or e-mail someone in prison. I'm going to see him on Friday. I don't want to give him false hope. Not yet."

Pascal wrinkled his nose. "You're not sure?"

She found the question irritating. "It's not about being sure or not sure. This stuff is key but I need to have it in full before we go to the police. I want to go to them in the sure and certain knowledge that this proves that, at the time the money was being physically taken out of the bank, Morris Walker was sitting in a café near Tower Hill eating a ham and mushroom bruschetta."

Pascal stroked his chin in thought. "Of course, if the police..."

"If the police what?" she said.

"If the police are now investigating Paul's link to the stolen money, this throws things into a new light."

"Does it?"

"The person who attacked me at Grove End studios. I don't remember much, but I do remember them saying 'Give it to me. Give it to me.' I had nothing to give them. I didn't know them. But what if they didn't know I wasn't the person they were after? What if it was mistaken identity?"

"It's a possibility," she said. "But what has that got to do with Morris?"

Pascal cocked his head. "What if Paul was the person they were really after? What if the 'it' they wanted was the stolen money?"

"Yes?"

He looked her in the eye. "What if Morris Walker and Paul Kensington were in on it together all along? They stole the money together. Morris could well have his cockamamie alibi if it was Paul Kensington in the bank that afternoon."

Chapter Thirty-One

Zaf and Newton bustled around the depot getting the two cats ready for their recording session. It was good to be doing something productive when they could feel their working world crumbling about them.

They had got both cats into their carriers and were waiting for the taxi to pick them up. The carriers were on chairs, separated by a good few feet, and Newton strode between them, addressing the cats.

"Today you have the chance to achieve stardom," he said. "You both have amazing qualities and we want to give you every opportunity to demonstrate them to the world. That means you both need to keep your eyes on the prize and not be tempted to behave in a way that lets us all down. Gus, that means you need to stay in the same place for the entire day. I know you like to explore, but we need focus. Understand?"

Gus gave a small *meep* of acknowledgement, as he often did when addressed by name.

"And Boudicca, you need to curb your most violent excesses. You have a beautiful singing voice, but to capture that we need to avoid destroying the equipment or maiming the humans. Think you can do that?"

Boudicca remained silent, glaring at the humans each time they dared to make eye contact.

"Yes, right. Good." Newton coughed. "I think the taxi's here. Zaf, you have the supplies?"

Zaf nodded. The most important thing in his bag was the deli salmon for Boudicca. He'd bought enough for Gus too, in theory. But it seemed more likely that Boudicca would just keep eating it until they ran out.

"Hey, Newton," said Zaf as they rode in the taxi. "If we gave Gus some of the salmon, would Boudicca get upset?"

Newton pulled a face. "I imagine she would. If we give some to Gus then we do it when she is not looking."

"Got it." Zaf hoped they could manage that. When had he become slave to a tempestuous cat diva? "What will happen to Boudicca after the recording?"

Newton glanced at the two cats and lowered his voice. "You do know we can't keep her in the depot, don't you?"

"Er, yes."

It had been difficult, keeping Boudicca isolated in Paul Kensington's office, trying to slip food in through the door without letting her out. She would try to bolt and was happy to use her teeth and claws on any hands that came through the door. Her reasoning – and its logic could not be faulted – seemed to be that if she sank her teeth into the hand that provided the food, then she could exploit that momentary weakness to slip through the gap.

"I can't see there's many choices," said Newton. "If she goes to the cat shelter it'll bring out the worst in her. Nobody will adopt a cat that flings herself at the window, snarling at passers-by while she stares at them with murder in her eyes.

She might be better off if we put her back where we found her."

"Back in Baker Street station?" said Zaf. "Surely not? There has to be something better than that?"

Newton gave a forlorn shrug. They were out of ideas.

Chapter Thirty-Two

Diana left the hospital, planting a kiss on Pascal's cheek and telling him she'd see him again soon. As she stepped outside, she found she had a message from Chaz, asking whether she'd be willing to help look through some of the old demo tapes at the studio. It sounded like an excellent way to occupy her mind, rather than dwelling on the misfortunes of Chartwell and Crouch.

A visit to Abbey Road would also allow her to get hold of Zaf and Newton one last time before Rita de la Cruz's visit and instil in them the need to make a good impression. She'd already had messages from Zaf assuring her the depot was as ready for inspection as it ever would be.

It was half an hour's walk to the studio from the hospital, but she decided to make a detour via the depot for a change of clothes. She switched into jeans and an old sweatshirt, assuming that she might need to delve into filthy cupboards to look through old tapes. She then walked from the depot to St John's Wood and Abbey Road.

Chaz was in the *Let it Bean* café in front of the studio.

"Oi, oi," he called as Diana entered. There were two waiting staff dealing with the small number of afternoon customers and Chaz wandered over to greet her. "Not been driven away permanently by last Friday's shenanigans?"

Diana wasn't sure if she'd have described a brutal assault and a murder as 'shenanigans' but didn't say so.

"Thanks for helping with this, anyway," he said. "There's a ton of stuff in the old studio, but I need a little bit of expert help to know what it is I'm looking at. Ken said you two used to understand the notation they used on the tapes."

"No problem, Chaz. To be honest, the distraction is welcome. I've also heard interesting things about the cat album being recorded."

"Oh, yes." There was a cheeky look in his eye. "Ken is definitely in the zone. Even a broken shoulder hasn't slowed him. You want to go in and see?"

"That was my intention."

He undid his apron and tossed it over the counter to a woman who caught it deftly. With a tilt of his head, he indicated for Diana to follow him.

"So, is there still money in the recording business?" she asked.

"There is," he replied as they crossed to the Grove End Studios proper. "Not like it used to be. Actual record sales are less important. Streaming doesn't pay well for the bands or producers. The three areas I want to focus on are merch, vinyl and live gigs."

"And the cat album." Diana struggled to imagine a herd of cats – or whatever the collective noun was – performing live on stage together.

"It's our first recording project here. Call it a test of concept," said Chaz.

"An expensive one, surely?"

"Oh, it's fine. I've taken out insurance. If it all goes belly up, I can still recoup my losses."

Past the front office, they made their way along the corridor to Studio One.

"I saw a review... of your café," said Diana, trying to drop it lightly into the conversation.

The East End hard man looked at her. "Pascal's piece? I'm not gonna lie, it was a blow. We were so new and it felt like he was having a pop cos we're not as upscale as he'd like."

Diana could imagine snobbery playing a part. Pascal was someone who, despite his fine qualities, enjoyed the trappings of wealth and success. Perhaps being drawn back to leaner times bothered him.

"Anyways, it turned out he didn't really make much of a difference to us," said Chaz happily. "Most of our customers come in off the street while they're here looking at the Beatles stuff. They're not here cos of the reviews."

Zaf and Newton were in Studio One, along with Ken Ferrari. The brace and sling on his arm looked bulky and uncomfortable, but Ken moved with his usual carefree energy.

"Hey. Come to see the magic happen?"

"Something like that," said Diana. "Where are the cats?"

Newton pointed at two recording booths.

"The two of them are in different rooms?" said Diana.

"Oh, yes. We heard that message loud and clear," said Ken. "And we got the riders as requested."

"Riders?" said Diana.

"List of likes and dislikes," said Zaf.

"I know what riders are," said Diana. "I meant, do cats have riders? Can they?"

Newton looked evasive. "We want to bring out the best in our stars, don't we?"

Newton was well known for indulging Gus, possibly more than was strictly necessary. "What sort of things did you put down, Newton?"

Ken beckoned her over. "Come and see. We can let our stars relax in their own immersive environments."

"Here's Gus's pad," said Chaz with a flourish as he opened the door. "See how we've installed a kitty play area with swinging toys, scratch posts and soft bedding on multiple levels. Now you said he's smart, do you think he'll work out this catnip dispenser?" Ken leaned over to demonstrate. "See this button? He presses this and it'll chuck out the good stuff." The dispenser was roughly the size and shape of a blender. Diana could see catnip in the upper portion, inside a container made from red translucent plastic. It looked oddly familiar.

"Is that one of those old-fashioned kitchen tea caddies?"

"It is indeed!" said Ken.

Gus was over by the catnip, purring with happiness.

"I think Gus will love it in here," said Diana.

"Nice." Ken beamed with pride. "Shall we move on to Boudicca's studio?"

They closed the door on Gus, who was now chomping catnip and rolling on his back in delight.

"Now Boudicca's needs are a little different, according to Newton's list," said Ken. He tapped on the glass of a very different space. "Here the lighting is darker and so are the amusements. We've installed a greyhound lure for her to chase." Ken picked up a plipper. "See this? When I press the button, the lure shoots round the wire, which takes in the whole room." He held down the button and with a high electrical whine, something looking like a white mop head shot across the room, turned a corner and made a circuit.

The dark shadow that was Boudicca lunged forward, desperate to catch the rapidly moving lure.

"Where do you even get a thing like that?" asked Newton, crouching to examine the mechanics of the device.

"I've got a diverse portfolio, mate," said Chaz with a wink. "Dog track over in the east."

"You've made her some high shelves and ropes to climb as well. Perfect," said Newton.

"We modelled it on the tiger enclosure at Regents Park Zoo," said Ken. Diana had no idea whether he was joking.

"So the cats each have their studio and the orchestra will be in another one," said Ken.

Diana looked at the lengths the producer had gone to, to make the cats feel at home.

"This is..." She wanted to reach for a word that wasn't 'insane' or 'a terrible business idea', and settled on "innovative. This is an innovate and thoughtful solution."

"I knew you'd like it," said Ken.

"Anyway," Chaz said to Diana. "Shall I show you two where the tapes and things are?"

Diana frowned. "What do you mean by 'you two'?"

"You and Ariadne. I thought I said?"

As Diana turned to look at Chaz's face Ariadne walked into Studio One. She carried a cup of takeout coffee and wore a smart suit with high heels. Not exactly tidying and rummaging gear.

"Well, hello, Diana. I see you've adopted a casual look today."

Diana wanted to elevate herself above any snide

comments. "Not all of us wear clothing as a defence, Ariadne. I'm happy to dress appropriately for the task in hand."

Ariadne gave Chaz a questioning look.

"If we're diving into dirty cupboards, we don't want to snag our expensive tights, do we?" said Diana.

Ariadne smiled broadly. "Well that's super! Did you hear that, Chaz? Diana has volunteered to dive into dirty cupboards. I will be able to sit back and offer my personal insights. Now that's what I call teamwork."

Chapter Thirty-Three

Diana fumed silently as Chaz led the way out and up the stairs to the studios in the floors above. An afternoon spent looking through old recordings was one thing. Being forced to do the same thing in the company of the snippy and sarcastic Ariadne Webb was something else entirely.

She was surprised when Chaz ultimately stopped outside Studio Three on the top floor.

"But this is where...?"

"This is where Pascal was attacked," said Ariadne, sounding equally surprised.

"I thought you were alright with this," Chaz said. "It's where we've been storing old things."

"Of course, it's fine," said Ariadne.

Chaz used his master keys to open the door.

Diana hadn't retained much of an idea of what had been in here the other day. Her mind had been on Pascal.

Studio Three was by far the snuggest and most crowded of all the studios. Black curtains lined one wall while a herd of microphone stands and instrument cases leaned against another. The control room was little more than a corner of the room walled off with boards, the one booth likewise. Large speakers were set up and plugged in outside the booth, and storage cupboards lined another wall. The broken window by the fire exit had been boarded up but not repaired.

Diana and Ariadne looked at the faded brown stain on the bare floorboards.

"Is that where...?" asked Ariadne.

"It's where he fell," said Diana.

Being at the scene of the crime, nothing new struck her. Everyone had been downstairs. Pascal had come up here in search of old demo tapes. Zaf had returned from the roof after making a phone call to Alexsei and then told Paul to go up there if he needed to take a call.

Had anyone known who Paul had been talking to on the phone? That person might have heard Paul in his final moments, might even have heard his killer. She made a mental note to ask Sugarbrook if she saw him again.

And then the shouting and banging had started up from Studio Three. She and Ken and Tom Griffin had gone up with Zaf, who had then run downstairs to access the second floor fire exit via the fire escape. Then the disaster had unfolded. Pascal was struck over the head, the window smashed, and Paul fell to his death. It was only moments later that Diana, Tom and Ken were in the room and, far below, Newton, Ariadne and Chaz were seen at the rear doors of the studio.

It seemed incredible that anyone had the chance to escape from the scene in that time. It was barely enough time to throw away or conceal the hood that had covered the attacker's face.

Chaz could see the sombre looks on their faces. "He's going to get better though, isn't he?" he said.

"Out of hospital any day now," said Diana.

"I thought they were letting him out today," said Ariadne.

"There you go." Chaz nodded. "All is well. How'd you meet him, anyway?"

"Oh," said Diana. "Well, we met him a really long time ago."

"*Long* time ago," said Ariadne, laughing. "It was in Belgium, wasn't it?"

"It was," said Diana. "It's always a strange thing when you meet people abroad. If they're from your country, your city, there's an automatic kinship."

"It was in that gorgeous auberge. Cheap moules-frites, great beer. Everything you wanted if you were travelling."

"That and George Harrison."

"Sorry?" said Chaz. "You met George Harrison in Belgium?"

Diana raised an eyebrow. "He was a regular there. In fact, it was George that introduced us to Morris and Pascal."

Ariadne nodded. "George was genuinely interested in other people. He knew we were both interested in a career in music, and he insisted that we talk to these two chancers from our home town. What a guy."

Chaz shook his head. "I can't believe it. George Harrison."

"A defining moment for us," said Diana. "He made us talk with Pascal and Morris. He knew Morris as an up-and-coming producer. On top of that, back in London, George set us up in digs, so we could concentrate on our work."

"It was like a mini artists commune back in the day," recalled Ariadne, with a smile. "Dozens came through that Eccleston Square house. We were the ones who stayed there the longest though, weren't we? Especially you, Diana."

Ariadne's face took on a sad look. "I mean, it was a horrible thing that happened to you recently. Really horrible."

Diana gave her a nod of appreciation. Any sympathy from Ariadne came as a warming surprise.

Chaz made an effort to look sad for a moment, but he couldn't stop himself grinning. "What a life the two of you were living. Back then I was just tooling around the East End thinking I was gonna maybe get me own taxi one day."

"That's the fun thing about life," said Diana. "You never quite know where it's headed next."

Chapter Thirty-Four

"This is jolly," said Ariadne as they made a tour of the studio, noting where there were stores of tapes. She made a list on her tablet and slapped a yellow post-it note onto each cupboard with a number for reference. "Doesn't it take you right back, Diana?"

Diana nodded and touched an old push-button landline phone. "You ask people what they remember from the eighties and they'll say stuff like Rubik's Cube, but these lamps where you touch them and dim the light are one of the things that we all went mad for." She batted the base of a lamp in the corner to show what she meant.

"We're gonna get some of them rock salt lamps for ambient lighting," said Chaz. "Apparently the bands all love them cos they're mindful or summat."

Once the two of them had finished their circuit of the studio, yellow post-it notes were stuck on every door and shelf.

Ariadne held up the tablet on which she had listed each of those storage spaces. "We should make a start. Diana, do you want to bring out the tapes in cupboard number one? Probably best if I process them in one of the control rooms, then we can play them if we need to."

"I'll bring the first box," said Diana. She refused to accept that she was only good for fetching and carrying while Ariadne got the job of deciding what might be interesting or valuable.

She went to the first cupboard and dragged out a cardboard box. It emerged with several spiders and a good coating of dust. Diana wished she had a dustpan and brush, but didn't want to look any more like the hired help than she already did.

She carried the box, complete with its coating of dust and at least one spider, into the control room. She set it down on the low coffee table by the squishy vinyl settee where Ariadne had made herself comfortable. She couldn't help a fleeting moment of pleasure when Ariadne recoiled at the sight.

"Goodness, these have been squirreled away for a long time."

Diana lifted out some of the tapes, and the two of them studied the labels.

"So Chaz, Ken must have told you about the colour coding?" Ariadne said.

Chaz shuffled his feet. "He mentioned that session tapes have blue labels and production masters have green." He looked at the ceiling. "He also said something I didn't completely follow about formats and kilohertz."

Ariadne waved a hand. "The formats and kilohertz stuff is sound engineer detail for Tracy and Ken to worry about. So we have a mixture of session tapes and production masters in this box," she said. "See the labels?"

Chaz nodded. "Will they all be in playable condition? Ken seemed to think they might have deteriorated too much."

Ariadne shrugged. "These are probably not ideal storage conditions, but who knows?"

"Someone once told me that Robert Fripp, you know, from *King Crimson*, uses a chicken incubator to store his recording masters in a stable environment," said Diana.

"Quaint," said Ariadne.

"So what is on the tapes?" Chaz asked. "Like which band? It looks like '*Gorg Alien Doll*'."

"There was never really a convention for how they would lay out the band's name," said Diana. "At least not as far as I know."

She looked up at Ariadne, who nodded. "We have to try and figure it out."

"You know what would help a lot?" Diana said. "The booking records. If there's a log of who was in the studios on a particular date then it would be so much easier."

"You're right, Diana. I'm gonna go and have a shuftie, see what I can find." Chaz disappeared.

"We have no idea who '*Gorg Alien Doll*' was, do we?" said Ariadne.

Diana shrugged. "They might have been an obscure band that sank without trace. Gorgeous Alien Dolls, maybe? Not a name that rings a bell. I wonder which of the tapes Pascal was going to look at when he came up here last week. There's none out, are there?"

"Maybe he didn't even get a chance," said Ariadne. "Why don't you fetch another couple of boxes Diana? I will sort these out."

Diana's eyes narrowed. "You're not just going to glance through them and see what might be of interest to you personally? Obviously you will transcribe each label to make a catalogue?"

Ariadne huffed. "I suppose I could do that. It will help Chaz to know what he has in here, if nothing else."

Diana brought another box through and dumped it on the side, then decided she might as well bring a couple more. Each time she put a box down, a cloud of dust puffed out, and Ariadne waved a hand in irritation.

"What would be the best thing for us to find?" Diana asked, opening another box.

Ariadne considered the question. "From a personal point of view or from a pop history point of view?"

"Either."

"From a personal point of view, there might be some of the demo tapes we did. What would be your favourite thing to find?"

Diana looked over the unopened boxes. There were dozens more like these in the various cupboards, all filled with the creative outpourings of musicians from the past few decades. "We've got a whole load of hopes and dreams right here. Imagine how many people have been involved in making all this music. Having said that, it would be fun if we found something by one of the really big acts, wouldn't it? A forgotten gem left behind by Freddie Mercury maybe."

"He was here once, remember?"

Diana nodded. "Imagine if there were photos from back then, that would be something. If we found a photo that showed us in here with Freddie then I'd be bowled over."

"Yeah! Listen, why don't you sit in here and help me do the catalogue for a while?" said Ariadne. She didn't meet Diana's eye, but they both knew it was a concession, an olive branch of sorts.

"I will," said Diana.

It was as close as they would get to a co-operative truce.

"Go on then," said Diana, gesturing at the mixing desk.

"Cue up one of the tapes. Let's have a listen to what we've got here."

It took them a while to get one of the old tapes onto the reel-to-reel machine above the mixing desk. They were both rusty and there was much getting in each other's way before the tape was threaded through the head and up onto the other reel.

"It's all on little data cards now," said Ariadne. "Far less fiddly."

"Thank goodness."

"And now," declared Ariadne, "for the first time in decades, I give you the *Gorgeous Alien Dolls!*"

She set the tape rolling. From speakers inside and out, there was a crackle of dust, the click of drumsticks, and then a long discordant bout of screaming and guitar thrashing. It was so loud, Diana wouldn't have been surprised if it had been heard throughout the building.

They almost fought each other in their haste to turn it off.

"Yes, well..." said Ariadne in the silence that followed.

"Quite," said Diana. "Maybe not all music from the past needs to be rediscovered."

"Our fourth album, you mean?"

Diana both smiled and recoiled. "Did we really do a cover of *Stand by Me* on that album?"

"The whole thing, beginning to end, was a crime against music."

Diana laughed. "We had the arrogance of youth and the record label breathing down our neck. We thought that synthesisers and high energy improved everything."

"A shocking embarrassment of a record."

"Pascal was at his very worst at that point. Did we somehow not know about his drinking, or did we just not care?"

Ariadne sat back in thought. "We were living in a bubble then. A rock and roll bubble. Reality seemed so far away. Pascal was fuelling his creativity with drink and... and I'm not sure the rest of us were much better."

"We're older and wiser now, eh?" said Diana.

Ariadne's eyes glittered with amusement. "Older definitely. I don't know how wise either of us has ever been. Morris was the only one who ever profited long term from our business."

"Always the canny business mind," Diana agreed.

Chapter Thirty-Five

Zaf surveyed Studio One. The cats had settled in happily.

"Did you really say there was going to be an orchestra?" he asked Ken.

"Of course," said Ken. "They're in Studio Two, setting up. I've got a vision, and it's a big one. No expense spared from our man, Chaz." Ken stretched his arms up to the sky. "Your two cats have really brought this project to life. We have the light and the dark. The yin and the yang. Gus is our warm, glowing comfortable friend who likes to lie in the sunshine. His music will be warm and dreamy, or sometimes cheerful and upbeat."

"Sounds like Gus," said Newton.

"Whereas Boudicca is a creature of the darkness. Complex, mysterious and compelling."

Ken's arms sketched out the huge rollercoaster journey that his listeners would be taking.

"Cats and people will listen to this music together. Sometimes they will relax in the sun, sometimes they will prowl along the rooftops."

"It sounds amazing," said Newton. "Do we need to do something special to get the cats to go to their microphones?"

Ken shook his head. "Those microphones are super sensitive. If they make a peep anywhere in the room we'll pick it up."

Zaf and Newton sat drinking tea on the squishy settee while Ken and Tracy Chen worked at the control desk. The orchestra were setting up in Studio Two. Chaz had come down to join them. Tracy worked to optimise the sound from each microphone while Ken directed everybody and Chaz watched over them all like a proud father. There was a camera feed from each studio room as well as the audio feeds.

"We'll work with Gus while he's enjoying the catnip, I think," said Ken. "That lovely soft motorbike purring puts me in mind of the bass line from *Get Ready* by The Temptations. Hear it?" He wagged a finger to a rhythm that only he could hear. Tracy nodded and her hands whizzed across the controls. Chaz stood, hands in pockets, grinning at the process.

Zaf racked his brains and plucked what he thought was the right song from his memory. He had no idea what the bass line sounded like. Based on Newton's face, the cat was going through the same mental process.

Ken had moved on. He'd sampled Gus's purring and was talking into his headset, asking the brass section of the orchestra to play some complementary flourishes. The sounds were fed through into the mixing desk and, when Ken tapped a button on his headset, audible throughout the room. A few minutes later, it was already starting to sound like a gently rousing song. The sort of thing that reminded Zaf of being outside early on a beautiful sunny day.

"This is nice," he whispered to Newton.

Newton nodded. "It's very Gus."

Zaf was in awe of Ken's skills and vision, but also slightly bored as they circled around some of the finer details multiple times, trying to get things exactly right. He found himself thinking about Paul Kensington and Pascal being attacked in this very place.

As a thought experiment, Zaf wondered whether they should be looking at Diana as a potential suspect. He felt guilty even for considering it. But she'd had a difficult relationship with Paul Kensington. What about Pascal? She was always civil to him, but everything about Diana's history with her music industry colleagues was murky and complicated. Maybe he would ask Newton if he knew more.

Newton was absorbed with Gus's performance.

"Let's take five," said Ken. "Then we're going to see if we can lay down some of Boudicca's bits."

"I might pop in and see Gus," said Newton. "He's done so well, he deserves a bit of fuss."

Zaf smiled as Newton hurried off to find his best friend.

Gus sat on Newton's lap as Ariadne and Diana entered the studio.

"All done sorting old tapes?" said Chaz.

"We've made some headway," Ariadne replied, "but my old friend Diana here needs a bit of a rest."

"I'm exactly as old as you, you fool," said Diana.

Ariadne smiled. "It's the wear and tear though, not the years. I thought I'd come to spend a little time with Boudicca. She responded well to my last intervention, so maybe I can charm her into singing for us today."

Zaf glanced at Diana and wondered what she thought about Ariadne sidling into the new recording project. Would it bother her that she hadn't been offered the same opportunity?

"I'll pop in there and see what I can do," Ariadne continued. "Ken's run through some ideas he wants to try. I'm sure that with a little coaxing, that cat will be a star."

"Wait!" said Chaz. "Yer'll want the plipper."

"The what?"

Chaz showed Ariadne the tiny device that would make the greyhound lure zoom across the room. "Yer might need it if she gets feisty. Be a good distraction."

Ariadne looked around at them all. "You all act as if she's an absolute monster. She's just a cat!"

"I mean, she is a bit of a monster," said Diana.

Newton pulled up his sleeves and showed her the scratches on his arms.

"Pfft. Well, if you're going in there with an attitude like that, then who can blame her?" Ariadne made her way to the studio with Boudicca.

In the control room Zaf crowded behind Ken and Tracy to watch Ariadne with Boudicca on the monitor. As Ariadne entered, Boudicca adopted an aggressive stance, hair on end, back arched. Ariadne walked over to her and swept her up into an embrace. Zaf could almost feel the scratches in his own arms. Did ACE Tours equip their staff with body armour or something? Ariadne was acting as if there wasn't a monster cat shredding her arms.

"I'm going to sing some scales while she settles down."

Ariadne began to sing scales. Her singing wasn't punctuated by the shrieks of pain Zaf had expected.

"I think she likes it," said Ariadne. "Now, I will see if I can do some call and response with her. Miaow!"

Boudicca responded with her own loud miaow. Ariadne repeated the same thing and Boudicca began to look pleased with herself.

"Love it, darling!" shouted Ken. "It's like Kate Bush doing the Hounds of Love, but with a cat!"

"Let's see how high she can go." Ariadne pitched her miaow progressively higher to see if Boudicca would follow suit.

"What a beautiful voice she has," said Ken.

The sounds the cat was making reminded Zaf of the eerie noise that tube trains sometimes made when they were accelerating. Had Boudicca learned how to emulate the sounds of the underground?

"Ariadne, darling?" Ken was using the intercom to the studio. "Thank you for warming her up. Now, if we play specific notes, let's see if Boudicca can match them. It would be so good if we could capture each one."

Ariadne stayed silent while Ken played sounds to Boudicca. The cat responded by making sounds that were clear and haunting as they emerged from the speakers.

"Gorgeous, just gorgeous," said Ken. "Now I have a good range of samples for the rock opera tracks. I'm already thinking that we can call this one *Lament for the Midnight Mice*. Can you hear the aching of her heart?"

Zaf closed his eyes. Boudicca's voice was so clear, so intense. It really did seem like she was trying to communicate with them. Was she lamenting midnight mice or just promising to scratch them later?

He turned to Newton. "Can you hear the aching of Boudicca's heart?"

Newton's brow furrowed. "I think that maybe I can hear Boudicca asking for fresh salmon."

Chapter Thirty-Six

Two hours spent in the recording studio confirmed several things in Diana's mind. Watching the slow, sometimes tedious process of adjusting equipment, checking levels and prepping for recording, she was reminded of how much time went into the act of recording. What had been true for her as a vocalist in the eighties was still very much true now. She saw, too, that Ken Ferrari, however mad his pet project might be, was utterly devoted to getting the very best from his artistes.

It was also quite clear, at least to Diana's ears, that cat vocalists were never going to produce popular hits.

Ken and his sound engineer, Tracy Chen, worked into the evening with utter concentration. Newton and Zaf seemed perfectly happy to sit around and watch. Zaf even took a call from Alexsei and said he'd be late home for dinner. Watching cats singing was apparently that entertaining.

But Diana needed to get home and rest if she was to prepare for Rita de la Cruz's company audit in the morning.

With a fond farewell to all and even a wave to Ariadne through the booth window, she slipped out of Studio One.

Frustrated at having only questions and no revelations, Diana went downstairs and out into the London evening. Her route home brought her almost immediately to the famous Abbey Road zebra crossing.

The zebra crossing on the front cover of the *Abbey Road* album, featuring the Beatles walking across it with their exaggerated strides, had become an accidental icon. It was always busy with tourists recreating their own versions of the photo, but right now, Diana had it to herself. She walked out into the road, the traffic slowing and stopping for her as she crossed.

Just as she reached the halfway point, a car pulled out from behind the stationary one in front of it and accelerated straight at her. Diana froze, then teetered backwards in the nick of time. The car caught her handbag with a glancing blow, sending her spinning to the asphalt.

She looked up in time to see the little black car powering away down Abbey Road.

People emerged from their vehicles to assist.

"Are you OK?" asked a man.

Diana pushed herself up to a sitting position. She felt oddly embarrassed. Would someone younger have been able to dodge out of the way more quickly?

"I think so."

"Take my hand if you feel steady enough to get up." The man had a kind voice, but Diana barely registered his face. She needed to get somewhere, to sit down and recover.

"He didn't see you," said a woman.

Diana frowned.

That wasn't true. That wasn't true at all.

"Do you know him?" asked the man. "He was driving right at you."

"He was," she murmured.

The man's face was full of confusion. "Does someone want to kill you?"

Chapter Thirty-Seven

"Where's Gus?" asked Zaf.

He'd been engrossed in Ariadne's work with Boudicca. Now he, and Newton, too, had failed to notice that Newton's lap was empty.

"I don't think he enjoys Boudicca's singing as much as Ken does," said Newton. "He's stretching his legs."

Zaf looked around. No sign of Gus. He fixed Newton with a firm look. "We need to keep an eye on him. You know how he likes to go exploring."

"He won't have gone far," said Newton, getting up. "I'll go and have a look."

Zaf followed. "If we lose our diva recording star, his career may already be over before it's even begun."

They walked the corridors of the recording studio, peering into cupboards and making discreet *pspsps* noises.

"I heard something," said Newton from a kitchen at the rear of the building. He pointed at the wall next to a cupboard door. "In there."

Zaf shook his head. "I already checked in there. It's a bunch of boxes on shelves. No cat, I'm certain."

"I checked it too, mate, but listen."

A faint scratching sound came from the side of the door. Zaf held it open and examined the back of the cupboard. "That's odd."

Newton nodded. "The shelves only go back about eighteen inches, but the scratching's coming from further back."

They unloaded the boxes from the shelves and Newton shone the light from his phone onto the wall side of the cupboard. "There's a little tiny door behind the shelves. It's not even a door really, more like a hatch to get to the electrics or something."

They removed the hatch, which was a thin sheet of wood. Gus poked his head out of the cubby hole behind.

"Gus, you little tinker!" said Newton, grabbing him. "I have no idea how you got in there, but you're out now."

He peered into the hole the cat had come out of. "There are some other things in there." He reached in to pull out an archive box. It was like the ones that lined the shelves in other parts of the building, but even dustier.

"More old stuff for Diana and Ariadne to sort through," Newton grunted.

Zaf put the door back in place and reloaded the boxes onto the shelf. He left the dusty box on the floor in case anyone might be interested.

"Come on, let's get Gus back to where he's supposed to be," said Newton. "Before Ken realises he's missing."

Chapter Thirty-Eight

Diana sat on the pavement by the Abbey Road zebra crossing, her handbag clutched to her chest. Someone had pushed it into her arms.

The kind man stood in front of her. "We can call you an ambulance if you want."

Diana didn't want an ambulance. She wanted to get up onto her own two legs and get out of the way. Somewhere further back in the queue of traffic, people were tooting their horns.

"Pay no mind to them," said the man. "Take my arm, but only if you feel steady."

Diana took the stranger's arm and slowly stood. She looked around.

"Did you see the car that hit me?" she asked.

"Black Ford Focus, shot off up the road."

Once Diana made it to the pavement she started to feel more like herself, but she was still shaken. It took a moment to realise that Chaz Chase was now standing beside her.

"What the hell happened?" he said.

"Is she your mum?" asked the stranger.

Diana frowned. She was apparently a doddery old lady who shouldn't have been allowed to wander away from her 'son'.

"I think I'm alright," she said firmly. "But I wouldn't say no to a cup of tea and sit down."

Refusing all other offers of assistance, she nodded in thanks to the small crowd of onlookers and walked with Chaz back to the studio.

"You leave the recording studio for five minutes and this happens," said Chaz.

They entered the *Let it Bean* café, which was still doing a healthy early evening trade, and Chaz clicked his fingers at the waiting staff to bring tea to Diana. "You look white as a ghost, Diana."

Diana explained what had happened.

"That crossing is a nightmare," he said. "So many near misses happen there, it's ridiculous."

"I'm not sure that's what happened, Chaz."

"Nah, trust me. It's a busy enough junction without all the tourists larking about. People just lose their patience."

She shook her head. "Just for once, I was the only one crossing. And the car that nearly hit me, it wasn't even at the front of the line. It really did seem as if it was aiming straight for me."

"At least you'll be able to look it up on the webcam, eh?"

"Of course." She fished around for her phone.

A pot of tea arrived at her table.

"You need something sweet to restore the colour in your cheeks," said Chaz. "Now we have some fresh Here Comes the Sunflower Seed granola bars." He spotted her expression. "I have a feeling that granola bars won't cut it on this occasion. In that case I think I might recommend a Norwegian Woodland Berry cupcake."

Diana shook her head at the daft names. Puns did not a good menu make, although she didn't share Pascal's mean attitude towards the café's offerings. "Sounds good, Chaz. Thanks."

While Chaz went to fetch cake, Diana checked the webcam footage from the Abbey Road crossing. Chaz was right. It was a constantly monitored spot. If someone had chosen to mow her down deliberately, it was a foolish place to try it. Desperate, even.

After some searching, she found the video of her walking down the road, then stepping onto the crossing. All of the traffic was stationary. Then she saw the black Ford Focus nose out of the line of traffic and accelerate towards the crossing. It even turned slightly, in an apparent effort to hit her.

This was not someone who was just trying to get somewhere a little bit faster.

Chaz placed a brightly decorated cupcake in front of her and leaned over to peer into her screen.

"What do you make of it?" she said.

His face darkened. "That's bang out of order. Get the car details and me and Ernie will send some lads round to have a word with the blighter."

Diana winced. Any 'word' Ernie might have would be punctuated with heavy blows from a cricket bat or crowbar.

"Shame you can't read the number plate," said Chaz.

The number plate was obscured by Diana herself, initially, and then by her flying handbag.

Diana didn't enjoy watching herself on the ground with people fussing around her. It made her feel old.

"You got any enemies, Diana?" Chaz asked.

"Apparently, more than I realise."

She ate the cupcake slowly, but it was far too sugary for her taste. She sipped her tea with each mouthful and, while she contemplated what had just happened, she decided to follow up on a question that had been bothering her.

She had DCI Sugarbrook's number in her phone. She had met him before and had even had cause to seek his help in criminal matters. She did not know if he would be glad to hear from her.

"Miss Bakewell," he said. So he had her number stored in his phone, too.

"Hello, Detective Chief Inspector," she said. "I wonder if I could bother your brain for a second."

From behind the counter, Chaz squinted and mouthed a question she couldn't make out. He wouldn't be a fan of the police being contacted, even by phone, from his premises.

"Is this regarding the Paul Kensington murder?" Sugarbrook said.

"It is."

"You have further information to share with us."

"Not information. A question."

He sighed. "This is not how police investigations work."

"It's a very simple question, I assure you."

"Go ahead." His tone was taut.

"Just before he died, perhaps even while he was being pushed off the studio building, Paul was receiving a phone call."

"Yes," said Sugarbrook flatly.

"You know?"

"We do."

"Do you know who it was that called him?"

Sugarbrook did not answer for several seconds. "I feel I

should repeat, this is not how police investigations work," he said.

"It just crossed my mind..."

"And you didn't think it had crossed mine? Such a low opinion you have of me. But if you must know, the call came from the Grove End Studios."

"Pardon?"

"The call Paul received in the minutes before his death was from the switchboard within the studio. Potentially, from any of the landline phones that are connected inside the building. Now, you tell me, what does that say to you?"

Diana put down her cupcake. "Someone at the launch party phoned him."

"Probably."

"And..."

"Go on, Miss Bakewell."

"... it's possible that someone phoned him in order to get him to go out onto the fire escape where the signal was strongest."

"Which means...?"

She considered all the implications and then said, "Detective Sugarbrook. Clint. I feel I should report that I think someone just tried to run me over on Abbey Road."

"What?"

"You can check the webcam pointed at the Abbey Road crossing if you wish."

"Are you telling me someone has tried to kill you?"

"That might be the case."

Another sigh. "You know almost everyone at that launch party. Most of them knew Pascal or Paul or both."

"The killer is someone I know."

"Let's not jump to conclusions," said Sugarbrook.

"Assumptions are the enemy of truth. But I think you need to start thinking about who might wish you harm, and consider anything else you've not yet told me."

Diana's thoughts turned to her discovery of the café near Savage Gardens, and the fact that she potentially held the key to Morris's release from prison.

"I will tell you," she said. "Soon."

"Soon? Tell me what?"

She closed her eyes. The cupcake had brought on a sugar-rush headache.

"I need to sort through some things. In my mind, Detective. But I will have information to share soon."

"Whatever it is, you have a duty to tell me now."

"Soon, I promise." She hung up and pushed the remains of the cupcake away.

"What's the Old Bill got to say?" asked Chaz from behind the counter.

She smiled but did not answer the question. "I think I ought to get myself home."

"I'm driving you in my cab," he said. "And I'm not taking no argument from you."

Diana wasn't going to argue with him. It was a physical impossibility for Chaz to have driven that car and have then appeared at the crossing moments later. Whoever it was that had tried to kill her, it wasn't Chaz. She'd gladly travel home under his protection tonight.

And if he offered to have some of his thuggish associates watch over her and her mum that night, she wouldn't say no to that, either.

Chapter Thirty-Nine

Zaf was impressed.

Wiry old hippie or not, Ken had zestful energy for a man nearing seventy. The recording went on into the evening, and a number of orchestral session musicians came in to record their pieces to add to the curious ensemble of sounds. Zaf was beginning to grasp that the construction of a studio album was very much like one of Bev Bakewell's jigsaws. It was an ensemble of pieces, some of which were recognisable and obviously went well together, but also many that seemed odd and incongruous. It took the minds of Ken Ferrari and Tracy Chen to comprehend the whole, to know how it was going to all fit together.

The café in the front closed sometime after six, and Chaz had the day's leftover food brought through as a tea-time snack for everyone in Studio One. The coffee table was loaded with delicious sandwiches and baguettes. A pair of trollies held drinks and desserts.

Ken had rolled his eyes and called them lightweights for not working straight through, but that didn't stop him tucking in. Zaf ate a sandwich, but his eyes were already drifting towards the plate of *Long and Winding Rocky Road*. Some of the classical session musicians jostled each other and loaded up their plates as if free food was a rare and valuable treat. Perhaps for jobbing musicians it really was.

Ariadne left Boudicca behind in the studio and came out to join the others. "Hasn't she done well today?" she asked Zaf and Newton.

Zaf was trying to see how badly wounded Ariadne was, and he could see that Newton was doing the same. At first glance, she seemed unscathed, which was surely impossible.

"She has done well," he said. "She seems like a different cat with you, Ariadne."

"I treat her as an equal. I think that she and I are very alike."

Zaf tried to maintain a neutral and polite expression. This was dangerous ground to tread.

Newton had no qualms. "I guess you must be a bit alike, yeah."

"Thanks, Newton," said Ariadne. "In what way?"

Newton's eyes widened. "Oh... you know... lovely voice, a bit difficult to get along with at first—"

"Oh, you'll never guess what, Ariadne?" interrupted Zaf. "Newton and I found an old archive box in a cupboard. Well, it was Gus really."

Ariadne looked at the box and scoffed. "Dirty work. Diana and I catalogued all of those old archive boxes. I believe we counted one hundred and forty-five. It was a bit of a marathon."

"Well, Gus found the one hundred and forty-sixth," said Zaf. "It was in a weird little compartment back in the kitchen that you would never find unless there happened to be a cat stuck in it."

"How very interesting," she said. "I must take a look."

Before Zaf could show Ariadne the box, Ken clapped his hands and insisted that it was time to continue with the recording.

"We're going to need everyone to help with this next track." Ken was almost vibrating with a manic energy. "These two cats have inspired me so much. While you were all *taking a break*, I came up with a concept for a new track. It's going to be a jaunty marching song with Gus providing a toodle pip rhythm for us, while Boudicca sings a haunting solo over the top. In the meantime, I want as many feet as I can get into a spare studio so we can get a nice crunchy marching sound."

Zaf and Newton shrugged at each other. "We've got feet, we can help."

"What's a toodle pip rhythm?" asked Newton.

"No idea."

As they were being organised in front of microphones, Chaz sidled up to Zaf.

"Mate, can I ask you a favour?"

Being asked a favour by an East End criminal was not something Zaf enjoyed. "Er, what?"

"Keep an eye on your friend, Diana, tomorrow."

"What? I mean, sure. Why?"

Chaz tapped his nose. "I'm just saying. Keep an eye out for her, yeah? She's well loved, you know that."

"I do know that."

Zaf wanted to know more. But Chaz moved off and Ken began positioning people and giving out specific instructions.

Maybe things would become clearer tomorrow.

Chapter Forty

"Car's been parked there all night," said Beverley Bakewell the following morning.

Diana looked up from the toaster. "Come away from the curtain, I've made you breakfast, Mum."

"I think that's Kenny the Kite and one of the Hendersons."

"Toast, Mum."

"They're Ernie's lads, aren't they? Probably up to no good."

"Well, let's give them the benefit of the doubt, eh?" Diana reached for her recently ironed work jacket. "Eat your toast. We'll start a new jigsaw tonight."

She stepped out of their little flat and walked towards the tube station, sending a nod of acknowledgement to the two men who'd parked outside their home all night. They returned it in kind.

Diana had not slept well. Dozens of thoughts had swirled around her head, mostly about who might wish her harm, and what that had meant in terms of the murder at the studio. Clearly Chaz and Ernie had her back (unless they were playing some deeply convoluted long game) which meant they were not behind the attack on her and therefore, she hoped, were not behind the attacks on Pascal and Paul.

Sugarbrook's revelation that Paul had received a call from within the studio suggested that his death was no accident. If so, did that have something to do with the missing Chartwell and Crouch fortune?

She shook her head as she strode through the East End streets. She needed to focus on Chartwell and Crouch today.

Rita de la Cruz, the woman who would probably decide their future, was arriving this morning. If Diana was to do her best for Zaf and Newton and the depot itself, she needed to paint a positive and optimistic picture of their business.

Diana had absorbed most of Paul Kensington's plans and communications over the past days. It was depressing reading. What she'd really hoped for was some untapped resource, or some obvious oversight by Paul that would lead to an 'aha!' moment during which she might pull a couple of hundred thousand pounds out of the air and save Chartwell and Crouch from its inevitable fate. She had found nothing of the sort. Paul Kensington might have been a hopeless people manager and a barely competent businessman, but he had accounted for all of the money, and the fact of the matter was that it was gone. All of it. The problems that had begun with the fake ticket fraud had been the start of the company's financial decline, and a series of poor decisions had ensured that the company never recovered.

Just before ten o'clock, Rita de la Cruz stepped through the door into the depot. Newton had been cleaning the one remaining vintage bus for the past hour. Zaf had been given the task of looking busy on the phone, as though taking bookings.

Rita was possibly half Diana's age, with a serious round face behind studious spectacles.

"Rita de la Cruz, TripTastic Limited."

"Diana Bakewell, Chartwell and Crouch."

Rita shook Diana's hand and looked around at the cavernous space.

"Interesting that you're located so centrally," she said. "That can't be cheap, a big space like this."

"You are correct, it's one of the business's largest costs. We have a partnership deal with a nearby hotel, but the number of tours from that source have declined in recent months."

Diana wondered whether Paul had spotted the trend, and what he'd done about it. She had found no evidence that he had reached out to see what might be wrong.

"Of course, without your bus fleet you will have no need for this space," said Rita.

"Possibly true," said Diana. "But it doesn't have to be that way. Perhaps we could talk about the ways in which a future Chartwell and Crouch might operate?"

Rita gave her a curious look. "Lead the way. I'm keen to see what you have to show me."

Diana led her into the kitchenette. "I can show you the accounts and I can speak to the facts of what has happened here. What I am unable to represent is what Paul Kensington's thought processes might have been."

"Of course," said Rita. "Sorry for your loss."

She didn't sound at all sorry.

"Did you know Paul at all?" Diana asked.

"I met him," said Rita, "but only at the annual conference that we have for franchisees."

"Right. Because TripTastic is the parent company of Chartwell and Crouch, right?"

Rita wrinkled her nose. "Chartwell and Crouch Marylebone is the last surviving branch of the original Chartwell and

Crouch company. Founded in the nineteen fifties, I believe. But all the Chartwell and Crouch depots became independent franchisees of Fine Tours London Limited, which is owned wholly by TripTastic Limited."

"I think I followed that," said Diana.

"We perform very little oversight on individual companies. It's the uniqueness of each member of the TripTastic family that creates strength and longevity."

"In the case of Chartwell and Crouch, some oversight might have been a helpful thing," said Diana. "Maybe someone could have helped save us."

"Was Paul the sort of person who welcomed help?" asked Rita.

"No, not at all," said Diana. "Now, why don't I open up the accounts and put the kettle on while you browse?"

Rita navigated the documents presented on the laptop with practised ease, and fired questions at Diana, many of which Diana couldn't answer because Paul Kensington had taken certain nuggets of information to his grave.

Rita sipped her tea and continued to trawl documents. "Now, what can you tell me about the Londiniumarium?" Rita spoke the word carefully, frowning. "What a terrible name."

"You're not the first person to mention that," said Diana. "It was a project that Paul kept close to his chest until he suddenly decided it was time to start taking tour groups there. The idea, as far as I can tell, was to try and concentrate all of the experiences of London into a single concentrated dose, in an old converted warehouse."

"Yes," said Rita. "It sounded like a lot to try and squeeze into a single place. Was it well executed?"

Diana decided on full honesty. "It was a disaster. We had a group from the US, and Paul had us take them along to be the first customers. He called them VIPs but really they were guinea pigs. I think the whole place was staffed by people on minimum wage who hadn't been properly trained. My colleague Zaf got pulled in at the last minute to help them out. He still mutters darkly about the experience if you ask him. Our VIPs were subjected to a random ride on a fake tube train and then blasted with authentic smells from the Great Stink of the nineteenth century Thames. The combined effects made several people quite ill."

Rita pulled a face. "Remarkable. It looks like a terrible idea on paper, but from what you say the execution was possibly even worse."

Diana shrugged. She could vaguely hear Zaf in the next room, pretending to take phone bookings. "Paul was very committed to it."

"What a terrible shame. If it wasn't for that, we might have squeezed another year out of Chartwell and Crouch. It's lucky for everyone that someone wants to buy all of the assets."

It didn't feel lucky to Diana.

"All of the assets?" she asked.

"We've got an offer from ACE Tours."

"Tom Griffin? He's the one buying us out?"

Rita smiled politely. "You know Mr Griffin?"

"He's the owner of a company that's always been our rival," said Diana. "It's a double whammy for him, isn't it? He gets our assets and removes us from the playing field at the same time."

"It seems a sensible move on his part."

Diana nodded. If Tom was keen to buy off chunks of Chartwell and Crouch, Paul's death had certainly hastened the process. Was that motive enough for murder?

Chapter Forty-One

Zaf hovered outside the kitchen. Diana and the auditor woman, Rita, had been shut away in there for a very long time.

The implications of such a long discussion twisted Zaf's stomach in knots. He'd not yet had the chance to chat to Diana about Chaz's cryptic warning the night before. *Keep an eye on her?* The implication was that Diana was in danger.

How had she annoyed someone this time? Was it because she'd been asking too many questions about the attacks on Paul and Pascal? Was it because of her attempts to free Morris Walker from prison? Or had she found the inevitable evidence that Chaz's music studio enterprise was a front for something dodgier? Zaf had truly loved almost every moment of the recording process, but even he thought it seemed unlikely that an album of cat music was a serious proposition.

Newton rushed over to Zaf. "You'll never guess what!"

Zaf couldn't guess. His mind was full of other things.

"Er, you found a savings account you'd forgotten about and you're buying your own Routemaster?"

Newton looked wistful for a moment. "No. Even if I did find some spare money, apparently it's more important to get our roof fixed." He pulled a face.

"Some people have their priorities all messed up."

"They do! That was a rubbish guess by the way, try again."

"Oh, blimey. OK. You're moving to Wales so you can be closer to the textile mill that's powered by water?"

"No! No, but you're closer." Newton jiggled with excitement. "Remember that job I applied for with the looms?"

"I do."

"They invited me for an interview!"

Zaf raised an eyebrow. "In Shoreditch?"

"Yes! Can you believe it? They said my quirky application really spoke to them."

"That's amazing! I'm so pleased for you. When's the interview? We can spend some time preparing you."

Newton glanced up at the clock on the wall. "It's this afternoon. I'll need to leave soon. What preparation do you think I need?"

Zaf wondered how Diana would approach this. The number one thing she would caution against would be doing anything that would make Newton more nervous than he already would be. "Oh, nothing much, you know. Just make sure you don't have spinach between your teeth, and so on."

"Right." Newton gave him a giant, toothy grin. "Orl orrike?"

Zaf raised an eyebrow. "Then you'll be fine."

Newton nodded. "Listen. Have you talked to Tom Griffin about you maybe getting a job at ACE Tours?"

"No, not yet." Zaf didn't want to think about that, not while there was still hope for Chartwell and Crouch, however slender.

"Yeah, I get it," said Newton. "I mean, it might have been him that killed Paul Kensington."

"Er, what?"

"Strong possibility. All of this" – Newton gestured at the workplace around them – "it's all turned out in his favour."

"I don't think he murdered Paul," said Zaf.

"It would be pretty miserable if you went to work for him and then he ended up going to prison."

Zaf didn't like such thoughts. "Maybe Diana is saving the company right now. Thrashing out a deal that will throw a lifeline to Chartwell and Crouch."

Newton stuck his bottom lip out thoughtfully. "If anyone can, she can."

Perched on the bus's folding bonnet, Gus gave a considered yowl.

"Gus agrees," said Newton.

"I think Gus is just practising his cat-scales," said Zaf. "We've now trained him to be noisier. More yowls equals more treats."

Zaf stared at the kitchenette door as if the act of doing so might enable him to peer inside.

"I'm going to see what's going on," he said and strode over to the door.

"Don't interrupt them," Newton hissed.

"I'm just going to go in and be helpful," said Zaf with a wink.

He opened the door. Diana and the inspector, Rita, were looking over some plans Diana had laid out across the table.

"You've really clearly identified some market segments that are underserved," Rita said to Diana.

"Yes," said Diana as she pulled out a fresh sheet. "And here I've detailed some ways in which Chartwell and Crouch might create some attractive offerings, even without our trademark vintage buses."

Zaf quickly closed the door behind him. If Newton had heard that last remark, who knew how he'd react?

Diana looked up at him. "Everything alright, Zaf?"

"I just came in to see if you have everything you need."

Rita put her glasses back on to look at him. "Diana here had some absolutely marvellous ideas about things Chartwell and Crouch could have done to generate fresh revenues. I do like this idea of a variety of Beatles walking tours. Obviously, such things exist already, but if I'm not mistaken, Diana, you have close links to the music industry and even some connections to the Beatles themselves."

"I'm not sure about that..." Diana began demurely.

"She rented her flat off George Harrison," said Zaf. "Knew him personally."

"Fascinating stuff," said Rita. "I'd really like to look around the rest of the building. It's a huge space, a wonderful space, and I do wonder what the best use is to which TripTastic Limited might put it."

"I'll gladly show you," said Zaf.

It wasn't clear how poking round the warren of cupboards, corridors and hidden spaces in the depot might help Chartwell and Crouch turn a profit, but Zaf was sure that being keen to help could only score them brownie points.

Zaf gave Rita the super deluxe tour. The depot had plenty of little architectural quirks. Odd little rooms, many without windows. Cupboards boasting ornate woodwork, used to store leaflets and a few brollies.

"That back wall appears to be damaged," said Rita, pointing.

"Yes," said Zaf. "It actually leads to a series of small tunnels going down into Baker Street underground."

"Does it really?"

"Yes. We had a cat visitor use it more than a few times."

"Yes, I see you seem to have a permanent cat resident."

"Ah, that would be Gus," said Diana, following behind. "Something of a workplace mascot."

"We're such a great little company, even the animals love being here," said Zaf.

"What's up there?" asked Rita. She was pointing at the set of metal stairs leading up towards the dark space under the depot roof.

Zaf knew that Newton had taken over that attic-like space for his personal projects. Up there were his beautiful if idiosyncratic models of London landmarks and some mechanical marvels, mostly constructed from vintage metal Meccano pieces. Fascinating though they were, Zaf wasn't sure they'd count in their favour.

"There's nothing up there," he said. "Just dirty storage space. We never use it."

"Well, let's have a quick peek then," said Rita, and led the way up the stairs.

"I hope you've seen we're a keen team and ready to get Chartwell and Crouch back on the road," said Zaf.

Rita stopped at the top of the stairs and turned to face Zaf and Diana. "Can I be honest with you?"

"Please do," said Diana.

"If we'd been looking at this three months ago, or even six weeks ago, we might perhaps have made it work. I just think it's too late now."

"Really?" said Zaf.

"Chartwell and Crouch is approaching bankruptcy. There's no way to stop it."

"I thought you might say that," said Diana,

"Is there no hope at all?" asked Zaf. No one had actually said the word 'bankruptcy' until now, but it made sense.

"I don't think so, no. You and your colleague downstairs would be well advised to start looking around for other opportunities."

Zaf looked down from the staircase into the depot. Newton was crouched on the ground, giving Gus serious ear tickles and fusses.

"He's actually got a job interview this afternoon," he said.

"But selling off our final assets," said Diana. "Getting rid of the last bus. Who's going to tell him that?"

Rita pulled a face. "I think you know the answer to that, Diana."

Diana sighed. "I might need some time to build up the strength to do that."

"Take your time. I'd say you've got until the end of next week."

Zaf felt the air leave his body. "And there's nothing else to be done?"

"There's simply no money left," said Rita. She pressed on, pushed open the door to the attic space and said, "What's this?"

"Oh, I know what it looks like," said Zaf, wondering how best to explain Newton's many models.

But he realised, coming up behind Rita, that she wasn't even looking at the wider room. She was looking at a large holdall on the floor right in front of the door.

It was an old bag, the sort of thing tennis stars might have kept all their gear in before Zaf was born.

"It might be Newton's," said Zaf, knowing it wasn't.

He picked it up to move it aside. It was surprisingly heavy. With a curious grunt, he set it down again and unzipped it along its length. The bag practically sprang open under the pressure of its contents.

He heard a gasp.

It was stuffed with bundles of banknotes.

Rita was the first to speak. "Why are there thousands – er, thousands upon thousands of pounds, just sitting in your depot?"

Chapter Forty-Two

The police came down to the Chartwell and Crouch depot for the second time in as many weeks, this time in greater numbers.

DCI Sugarbrook stood in the attic doorway with the depot team and Rita de la Cruz gathered behind him. He looked at the big bag of banknotes.

"I don't jump to conclusions," he said, "but if I were a betting man..."

"You think that's the money defrauded from Chartwell and Crouch, don't you?" said Diana.

"But how can it be?" asked Zaf. "We've all been up here before and it's not been here."

"If we were to follow Detective Sugarbrook's line of thinking," said Diana, "that money was, until recently, in locker storage in a little place on Baker Street. I also imagine that Detective Sugarbrook expects the money found on Paul Kensington's body to match the money in the bag in terms of age and serial numbers or whatnot."

"Miss Bakewell likes to do the thinking on my behalf," rumbled Sugarbrook.

"But how?" asked Zaf. "Was Paul behind the fraud scheme?"

Diana raised an eyebrow. "He told me he didn't know anything about the locker key."

Newton looked puzzled. "But this is good news, right?"

Everyone looked at him.

He shrugged. "That's Chartwell and Crouch money, isn't it?"

"If it *is* the money in question," said Sugarbrook, "then that's money paid out by thousands of customers for tours that never existed."

"And for which Chartwell and Crouch had to pay them back out of its own pocket," Newton argued. "That's why we're in the hole we're in. We paid them back, so that's our money. We could buy back one of our buses, do a massive advertising campaign and buy a cat tree for Gus with the change."

Everyone was still staring at him. His cheek twitched. "We don't *have* to buy the cat tree."

"I'm afraid due legal process does not work like that, Mr Crombie," said Sugarbrook. "If what you say is right then that's stolen money and, therefore, it's evidence. Not to mention no longer being legal tender."

Zaf could see the crestfallen look drop onto Newton's face.

He followed the others to the stairs, reluctant to tear his gaze away from the huge pile of cash. Rita de la Cruz led the way.

"I'm afraid this changes nothing," she said. "If anything, this is the kind of negative publicity that seems to have hounded Chartwell and Crouch for something like a decade.

In my mind, it only reinforces the idea that this portion of the business needs to close its doors for good."

Zaf felt like she'd punched him in the gut.

Waiting for them on the ground floor were DS Quigley and a gaggle of uniformed officers, plus a couple of individuals in protective crime scene suits. After a nod from Sugarbrook, they headed up. Diana escorted Rita to the door and Zaf listened to their promises to keep communicating while Chartwell and Crouch slid inevitably to its demise.

He slumped against a wall, feeling flat. Newton was trying to stop Gus messing about with the crime scene equipment and photobombing the crime scene photos. Eventually it was time for him to go off to Shoreditch for his interview. Zaf took over cat-wrangling duties.

"I'll catch up with you later, find out how you did," Zaf said to Newton, waving him off. He turned to Diana. "This isn't a good day, is it?"

"Not the best of days, no."

"We seem to have nothing but bad days lately."

Diana looked at him and then put a hand on his. "I wouldn't put it like that."

"No? Our company has been given a death sentence. We've been given our marching orders. Your beautiful flat has been stolen from you and you're forced to live with your mum. And, on top of that, our boss has been murdered and your friend has been attacked. That's nothing but bad days."

"Or," she said, "we could consider that you are living in that lovely modern apartment with your rich and devoted boyfriend. My mum and me are getting to spend quality time together and almost coping with being under each other's feet. Newton is getting more fun out of Gus's 'singing career' than any man has any right to. The mystery of the stolen money is close to being solved, and when I see Morris tomorrow, I will be able to tell him that I have found several people willing to corroborate his alibi. Now *that's* all good news."

Zaf stared at her then sighed.

"Alexsei does love me, like crazy style," he admitted.

"See?" She patted his arm. "You should come with me."

"Where?"

"To see Morris tomorrow."

"I've never been inside a prison."

"There's always a first time."

"But why?"

"Because I want you there when I tell Morris the good news. You're a part of it, too. And I've mentioned you to Morris so many times, I think you ought to meet him."

Zaf was nervous of the prospect. Prisoners were scary people – right?

He laughed at himself. It was prejudice. Simple, ordinary, closed-minded prejudice. He'd been on the receiving end of it enough times in his life.

"I *will* come with you," he said.

"Good," said Diana.

"But first," added Zaf, "I want to know why Chaz told me to watch out for you."

"Pardon?"

He nodded. "Chaz seemed to think you were in some sort of danger."

She pursed her lips. *Don't lie to me*, he thought.

"Come on, Diana. Friends, huh?"

She nodded in acceptance.

"And maybe you can tell me about this person who apparently tried to run you over yesterday," said DCI Sugarbrook from behind them.

Zaf whirled. For a huge man, Sugarbrook could move quietly.

"How did y–?" Zaf glared at Diana. "Someone ran you over?"

"They failed, obviously," she said.

"Why didn't you...?" said Zaf, feeling very much out of the loop.

Diana looked around the depot.

"There's a lovely little café down the road that makes very tasty paninis," she said. "Let's talk there. This place is beginning to depress me."

Chapter Forty-Three

Tasty For You was an oddly named but rather good café not far from the bus depot. The owner, Levon, was a master of unassuming and polite service. Zaf wondered how this place would fare compared to *Let it Bean* if Pascal reviewed it.

Diana ordered a panini and Zaf agreed to share it with her. Sugarbrook simply ordered a black coffee.

As the order arrived, Diana recounted her near-death encounter on the Abbey Road zebra crossing.

"Blimey," said Zaf. "Like Paul McCartney."

"Pardon?" said Sugarbrook.

Zaf shook his head. "A car accident. The thing about the Abbey Road album cover being a coded message about Paul McCartney's death in a car crash."

"But he's not dead."

Zaf looked at him. "Ah, well, that's the conspiracy, isn't it? People thought Paul had died in nineteen sixty-six – car crash, a blow to the head – and had been replaced by a lookalike. John Lennon says 'I buried Paul' on the Strawberry Fields song track. The Abbey Road album cover is a funeral procession. The car on the street on the album has the registration '28IF' and Paul would have been twenty-eight *if* he'd lived. There's other stuff too. It's all there, plain as day."

"But Paul McCartney isn't dead," said Sugarbrook.

Zaf shrugged. "For some people the 'evidence' points towards him being dead even though he's perfectly fine and walking around."

Sugarbrook tutted. "We were talking about Miss Bakewell's accident which, unlike your urban myth, was very real. I looked at the CCTV footage. We've not been able to track the car. The driver deliberately obscured their registration plate with paint or mud. A dangerous tactic."

"I can't believe someone would try to kill you," said Zaf.

Diana looked down at her panini. "I'm struggling to believe it myself."

Sugarbrook put his hands together on the table, fingers interlaced like a stack of meaty sausages. "What do you know about the business dealings of Chaz Chase and Big Ernie Holland?"

Zaf looked at Diana, wondering what she could say.

"Let me rephrase," said Sugarbrook. "We all know that Chaz and Ernie are not honest businessmen. They are, at best, fraudsters and thieves and, at worst, the kind of old school London thugs who send people to the hospital with broken hands and dented heads. They are criminals. You know that."

Zaf focused on the panini.

"Life is complicated," said Diana. "People are not just one thing or another. I know who Chaz and Ernie are. You don't need to explain things to me."

Sugarbrook leaned in. "This latest 'business venture' by Chaz Chase, the recording studio. It's not going to be an up-front and honest business," he said. "The man has an angle. A tax dodge. Money laundering. I don't know. But the fact of the matter is, a serious crime was committed on those premises and I can't ignore the fact that men like Chaz Chase are willing to do all manner of dirty deeds to protect their sordid enterprises."

"Paul Kensington would never have been involved with that," said Zaf.

"I am willing to bet that Paul died with cash from a massive fraud on his person. Don't tell me he couldn't have been involved."

"But he's from a different world to them. He was like a stupid little puppy."

"And they're wolves," said Sugarbrook.

Diana exhaled softly. Zaf could see her fingers balanced on the edge of her plate.

"Chaz couldn't have been in the car that tried to run me over," she said. "It's not physically possible."

"He has men," said Sugarbrook. "His men have men."

"He came to my help afterwards, insisted on driving me home. He even had..."

Sugarbrook frowned. "What is it?"

She glanced at Zaf. "He had men parked outside my house all last night to make sure I was safe."

Sugarbrook looked at her. Even Zaf could hear how her words were not the reassurance she had intended them to be.

"I think you are potentially in a lot of trouble, Miss Bakewell," said the detective. "I urge you, not only as a police officer, but as someone who has a modicum of respect and affection for you, to tell me if there's anything else I should know."

She was silent for a long moment. At last she spoke.

"I have information about Morris Walker. Zaf and I are going to visit him at HMP Wandsworth tomorrow to tell him."

"What information?" Sugarbrook's voice was hard.

"It's about a Pomeranian called Marengo."

"What?"

"No, it's true," said Zaf. "It could change everything."

Chapter Forty-Four

As he was preparing to go home that evening, Zaf received a text from Newton.

Interview a complete bust. Drowning my sorrows.

Zaf sighed.

Where are you? he sent.

Howl in the Moon Pub, Shoreditch.

I'm on my way.

He found Newton perched on a stool by the bar, hunched over a half-empty glass. A folk duo were quietly playing in a corner. Zaf patted Newton on the back as he took the bar stool next to him.

"Whatever he's having," Zaf said to the barman. "Make it two. What are we having, Newton?"

Newton inspected his glass. "Ginger beer."

"Drowning your sorrows with non-alcoholic ginger beer?"

"I don't really drink."

"Two ginger beers, then," Zaf told the barman. He turned to Newton. "Tell me what happened."

Newton drew in a big breath like he was going to cry.

"They said looms," he said.

"They did."

"This place had looms, but they were more like kiddies' toys. Honestly, I'm not even joking. They look like someone took an old picture frame and put nails round it. The weaving part is done by hand, someone has to manually thread the weft through the warp. Madness! Apparently they're weaving old t-shirts into bathmats as part of a textile upcycling collective."

"That sounds... noble."

"They were hoping that I would come along and help them cut up t-shirts."

"I see," said Zaf. "Is the pay any good?"

Newton pulled a face. "It's a three month unpaid internship that might lead to a job that pays minimum wage."

"Ouch."

"It seems more like a hipster sweatshop. My skills must be worth more than that."

"They are, mate. Well, at least you got a chance to practise your interview skills."

The ginger beers were placed before them. Zaf thanked the barman.

"And we get to enjoy a nice pub in Shoreditch."

Newton gave a dramatic roll of his eyes. "Urgh! I hate this! Why can't things just be easy?"

"Pfft! Easy? I've seen you transform rusty spares that turn up in ropey packages into gleaming... um..." Zaf realised he had no idea what most of those things were. Every once in a while Newton would prance excitedly round the depot, crowing that he'd found a genuine vintage part, and it would turn out to be an unremarkable hunk of metal that looked as if it belonged in the recycling. "Anyway, whatever they are, you make them gleam, and what's more you make them *work*. Now that can't be easy. Most people could never do it."

"I know what you're trying to do, and thank you by the way," said Newton. "I just want to work on big old machines. It shouldn't be hard to find someone who needs to keep things going."

"Big machines, huh? You ever thought of working on the trains? The underground?"

"I've looked. I don't have the qualifications."

"Construction site machines."

"It's all too corporate and none of it's in central London."

Zaf nodded and sipped his ginger beer. It was sweet and tangy.

"I want something where I can work in a small team on something with a bit of character."

Zaf thought. "The Thames Flood Barrier."

"Looked into it. They're not hiring."

Zaf's mind's eye roved all across London.

"Escalators!" he said.

"Escalators? Like on the Underground? Ohh, interesting. There must be thousands of them all over London."

"And they're always breaking down," said Zaf. "Someone's got to fix them. What do they even look like underneath?"

"Well," said Newton, lost in thought. "I've never seen the workings, but there would have to be some kind of a drive train that moves the steps. Another one for the handrail, too. There will be a big motor somewhere."

Zaf was happy to let Newton speculate on the workings of an escalator for a few minutes, because it stopped him moping.

"Would it be a bit like being a mole, though?" said Newton.

"Sorry, what?" Zaf tuned back in to the conversation. "A mole?"

"If I spent all day every day working in dark compartments in the Underground, would I become like a mole, never seeing the sun?"

"Newton, I'm not sure it would be all that different from any indoor job," said Zaf. "When you're in the depot you don't see the sun."

Newton didn't look convinced.

"Do you think they'd let me bring Gus along?"

Zaf shuddered at the thought of over-inquisitive Gus among the world of escalators.

"Finding a job with machines that allows you to take your pet cat along might be a tall order, Newton."

Chapter Forty-Five

On Friday morning, Zaf caught first the tube and then the bus with Diana, out to south London and Wandsworth Prison. He still felt nervous, and the way the prison looked, like some creepy old castle, didn't help. But he went through, showed his ID, did as he was told by the staff, and found himself escorted through to the visiting room.

"Can I shake his hand?" he whispered to Diana.

"Pardon?"

"I don't know what the rules are about touching. Will they think I'm passing him drugs?"

She smiled. "Hugs and handshakes are permitted at the beginning and the end of the visit. Shake the man's hand. I'm sure he's keen to meet you."

The visiting room was a hall-like space with plastic seating. It reminded Zaf of parents' evenings at his old secondary school in Birmingham. They sat at a table and waited as prisoners in grey tracksuits entered.

The man who approached them was both older and younger than Zaf had expected. He was worn and lined with liver spots on his hands, but still had a kernel of youthful hand-someness. Zaf thought of his killer cheekbones on the Electra-Beat album covers.

"And who is this fine man?" asked Morris.

Diana hugged her friend then made the introductions. Morris's handshake was tight, hungry rather than dominating.

"Heard so much about you," said Morris and grinned.

"The same?"

"Oh, really?"

"I hear you're working on a stage production of 'Oliver!' with the guys here."

Morris nodded appreciatively. "It's coming on. Our Nancy is absolutely to die for. A few too many people fancied them-selves as Bill Sykes, especially since he doesn't have any singing parts, but I've coaxed enough of them into being Fagin's boys."

"Sounds good."

Morris grunted. "For a bunch of bank robbers and car thieves, they're surprisingly nervous. Push comes to shove, we might use a sound recording of the whole thing beforehand and then mime along after. It is what it is. However we do it, I'll wring the very best from them."

"You've still got showbusiness flowing through your veins then?" asked Zaf.

"Still do," Morris replied. "How was the Grove End Studios relaunch? Must have been magical."

Zaf looked at Diana, surprised that Morris didn't know it had been a complete disaster. But how would he have known? No phones in prison. No e-mail, no social media. Maybe a TV, and the good old fashioned grapevine of gossip.

Over the course of twenty minutes, Diana laid out what had happened that night. Morris appeared understandably shocked.

"Bloody hell," he whispered. "There was no love lost between me and Paul Kensington. No love lost between me and Pascal Palmer neither. But I wouldn't wish that on either of them."

"Quite," said Diana.

"You and Pascal not on speaking terms?" Zaf asked.

"We were the best of friends at one point. I was lead vocals in ElectraBeat, but together Pascal and I produced every single track the band recorded. We worked hand in glove. But then Pascal had his troubles." Morris mimed drinking.

"I know," said Zaf. "He sorted himself out in the end."

"It was a long journey," added Diana. "More than a decade lost to the booze."

"He drank away every penny he'd earned from our chart success," said Morris. "Beginning of the nineties, I saved my money, invested it, and offered to buy the rights to the Electra-Beat back catalogue from the others. Royalties were ticking over nicely enough but I suggested I could buy everyone else out for a decent sum. Thought it was a way of bunging Pascal and Ariadne a few quid without it looking like charity."

Diana eyed Zaf. "Morris is the hero of his own story here."

Morris shrugged with a smile.

"OK, OK. It was a savvy deal on my part," he said. "Ninety-five, Montell Jordan. You know him? *This is how we do it*," he sang. "Yeah. He sampled one of our tracks from the third album for his second single and that just went stratospheric. Made back my investment on the catalogue purchase within months. Everyone's happy."

"Not everyone," said Diana.

Another shrug. "Certain people weren't talking to me for months after that. I've not spoken to Pascal since. But he's been wrapped up in his own things – putting his life back together, his writing. I used those proceeds to buy into Chartwell and Crouch. Brought Diana along as my number one tour guide. How's the company going? Still limping along?"

Zaf puffed out his cheeks.

"That bad?" said Morris.

"The company has stopped limping," said Diana. "It has stopped. It's sitting on a comfy bench and waiting for the undertaker's hearse to take it away."

"Oh, hell." Morris sighed. "Newton must be gutted."

"I think he might still be in denial," said Zaf.

"It was a great company," said Morris. "And we had great times. If the walls of that place could talk, the tales they would tell..."

"About that..." said Diana. "We had a novel turn-up for the books yesterday." She told him about the bag of cash that had appeared in the attic space.

"But how?" asked Morris.

"That's the big question," said Diana. "I think the police's pet theory is that Paul Kensington was somehow involved in the fraudulent activity."

"Really? As in, I'm off the hook?"

"That's not part of their pet theory, I'm afraid," she said. "However, I have even more startling news."

"Blimey," said Morris, grinning. "This is too much for one day. You should spread this stuff out over multiple visits. What news?"

"I found Marengo."

The grin vanished from his face, replaced by stunned surprise.

"No. You kidding me, girl?"

"I am not kidding. I found Marengo and I found the café.

Hold on tight, because I also found an owner who quite possibly remembers you being there on the day in question."

And Zaf could see he *was* holding on tight. Morris's hands were bunched into tight fists on the table top between them, squeezing until his knuckles were pink patches on white fingers. His lips pressed together, he began to cry, silently.

Diana put her hand over his.

"It's great news," she said gently. "And, with your permission, I will talk to the police or a solicitor or whoever about what we do with this."

Morris Walker, tears on his cheeks now, gave small shaky nods of his head.

"There's a long road ahead of us yet," Diana continued gently, "but I think this could help us overturn your conviction."

It was no wonder the man was crying. The years he'd already spent inside for a crime that Diana was entirely convinced he did not commit. Those wasted years inside.

Of course, thought Zaf, if Morris was innocent, then the true culprit was still out there and roaming free. Or maybe it was Paul Kensington, laid out on a cold mortuary slab somewhere.

Chapter Forty-Six

Ken reckoned Gus and Boudicca needed only one more recording session to capture 'all of their majestic purrs and yowls'. And the three soon-to-be-jobless members of Chartwell and Crouch could think of no better way to spend their Friday afternoon than at the studio on Abbey Road.

Diana and Ariadne sat and continued sorting through boxes while Newton and Zaf encouraged the cats to produce the final sets of sounds that Ken demanded for his album. Chaz Chase came in and nodded appreciatively. Diana wasn't sure if he was hearing positive qualities in the cat recordings that she was deaf to.

As she watched Chaz she recalled Sugarbrook's words of warning. Chaz might appear to have her best interests at heart, but facts were facts. There was the cold heart of an underworld fixer in his chest.

Ariadne put down the last of the tape reels.

"I had expected – no, hoped – to find more of our old material," she said.

"I know," said Diana. "A chance to take a trip down memory lane."

Zaf turned to them. "You've seen the other box we found though, haven't you?"

"What box?" asked Diana.

He left the studio and returned with another dusty archive box.

"Found this in a little hidden cupboard in the kitchen out back," he said, presenting it to them.

"God, we used to just live in that kitchen sometimes," said Ariadne. "Work in here, eat in there. Did we ever go home?"

"How did you find this?" asked Diana, looking at the box.

"Oh, Gus found it while exploring."

"Imagine a cat doing a better job of finding archive material than us," said Ariadne.

"Everyone should have a sidekick cat," said Diana. "This is our stuff."

"Our recordings?"

"All our stuff," said Diana. She set the lid aside. "It's a real mixture. We have some tapes here, and some documents too. Let's have a look." She lifted out the top layer and spread it onto the table.

Ariadne picked up a tape. "This one might be interesting, it's one of our old demos."

"Hmm?" Diana glanced up from the document she was looking at. "That should be fun to hear, if it will play. Music from a bygone era."

"We're ladies of a certain age, not time travellers from the nineteen-twenties, Diana," said Ariadne. "You may be happy to be an old woman. I am not."

"All I'm saying is that this is a memento of the most marvellous time."

"That *is* true."

Newton, sitting nearby, made a noise. "I just don't get it. If you two were such good friends, why is it you're so weird with each other now?"

Diana watched Zaf's mouth drop open at the tactless question. She smiled as Zaf nudged Newton with his foot. Newton was oblivious.

Ariadne looked at Diana. "Yes, why are we 'weird' with each other now?"

"I'm sure most of the weirdness comes from you, Ariadne."

"Hardly!" Ariadne scoffed. "What's that phrase they always use in the music industry? We found that we had 'creative differences' or we were 'evolving in different directions, musically'." She mimed air quotes.

"Differences like what, though?" Newton asked. "In all the time I've known you, you've rarely had a nice word to say about each other. It's clearly not that you just didn't agree on some songs or whatever."

"Alright, well, here's my take." Diana looked over at Ariadne. "This all happened a really long time ago. We were doing well as a group. We had a string of singles, none as massive as *Count Me In*, but we charted with all of them. But then we had problems."

"Understatement," said Ariadne.

Diana ignored the interruption. "Pascal and Ariadne were together and Pascal... try recording a hit album every year and touring when the drummer-slash-producer spends most of his time lost to alcohol. After the fourth album—"

"A crime against music," said Ariadne.

"Catchy title," added Zaf.

Ariadne looked at him. "That wasn't the title. It was awful.

After that, Pascal and I went to the States for a time. I was seeking help for Pascal."

"Yes," said Diana, the scepticism evident in the single word. "Ariadne and Pascal spent a year in LA. While Pascal was drying out in a clinic, Ariadne had this idea that she could get a record deal for just her and Pascal. They would be the new Eurythmics, or the new Yazoo."

"That's a kind of milkshake," said Newton, frowning.

"Yazoo were a band. And like the Eurythmics, a male-female duo. Ariadne thought she and Pascal could go down that same path. She put more effort into furthering her own career than she did into the band."

"It really wasn't like that," said Ariadne.

"I've seen those photos of you poolside with American record label executives," said Diana. "You were making deals."

"I wasn't the one setting them up! Pascal had ambitions."

"He was doing group therapy in rehab or whatever."

There was a groan of annoyance. Diana looked up to see Ken Ferrari stomping over from the control room. He swung his arms as much as his shoulder sling would allow.

"Diana Bakewell! Ariadne Webb! If the two of you can't be civil in my dream factory then I must ask you both to leave!"

"We were being loud," said Diana. "Sorry."

"Loud?" he said. "You've been like this for forty years. Snippy, snippy, catty creatures. No, that's an insult to cats. Cats are delightful. They don't keep a pointless grudge going for decades." He flicked a finger between the two of them. "At least you've reminded me why ElectraBeat split up."

"Well, it wasn't because of us," said Ariadne. "It was a range of things."

"A range of things including the fact that you two couldn't bear to see each other happy. I think this is the most wonderful industry in the world, and I am grateful every day for the fact that we get paid to make wonderful music. But, you two... oh! You just had to keep scoring points off each other. Now be quiet, or buzz off!"

He stomped away again. Diana called out a heartfelt, "Sorry, Ken" after him.

Ken whirled. "And if you want to know the facts, you're both right and you're both wrong. Yes, Ariadne and Pascal *were* trying to score a separate record deal in the US, but it was Pascal who came up with the idea. Rehab, indeed! Even then he wasn't taking his drinking problem seriously. Took him another decade to get sober."

With that, Ken went back to his control room and slammed the door.

"Oops," muttered Ariadne.

"Is that true?" asked Diana. "About Pascal and the deal in the US?"

Ariadne nodded. "He was driving the whole thing."

"That's not what I remember."

"The rehab was a very obvious cover for us disappearing for a while. But we were both in LA, trying to get ourselves a deal as a duo."

Diana looked at the paperwork in her hand. "This box must have been one we squirreled away in the nineties. Look, a copy of the deal to sell Morris the back catalogue."

Ariadne grunted as she inspected it.

"A lump sum for us, and then Morris scores big when hip-hop artists start sampling our work."

"Lucky, I guess."

"Oh, now look at this," said Ariadne, pulling out another document. "The tenancy agreement to the Eccleston Square flat."

"Really?" said Zaf, scooting over.

"The very favourable rent agreement with Mr George Harrison."

"The contract where they diddled you out of your home?"

"The *original* agreement," said Diana.

"With my name on the bottom," said Ariadne, "because I wasn't afraid to put my name on the dotted line."

Ken came out, waving his good arm in the air.

"Have we annoyed him again?" said Diana.

But there was a smile on his face. "Tracy and I have agreed we need just one more take with our feline stars and then we'll be done with them."

"Done?" repeated Newton. He seemed crestfallen.

"One last rousing finale," said Ken, "and then Tracy and I can get down to the real business. The mixing of the masterpiece."

Diana exchanged looks with Ariadne. "Masterpiece," she said archly.

Chapter Forty-Seven

Zaf, Diana and Newton shared a taxi back to the depot on Chiltern Street.

Zaf and Newton struggled out first with their cat carriers. When Diana had joined them on the pavement, Newton pointed silently at the door. A sign was nailed to it.

This business has been acquired. It will be closed until further notice.

Diana tried the door, but it was locked. "How is this possible? There's not even a phone number to call." She rattled the door and gave it a slap with the flat of her hand, more to vent her frustration than in expectation of an answer.

Gus meowed in alarm in his carrier.

"What does it mean?" asked Zaf. "This is the end, right?"

"What about the cats?" said Newton. "It's their home. Gus's home, at least."

"I had hoped we'd get some genuine notice," said Diana. "But this looks like the end indeed. Shall we go and get a drink somewhere? I think we need it."

"Yes. Yes please," said Newton in a small voice.

"Good. And then we will work out what to do next."

"We're not going to forget the cats, are we?" said Newton. "Gus and Boudicca can't stay cooped up forever."

"They won't."

"Gus will come home with me, obviously," Newton added. "My house is no bus depot but at least it's somewhere."

Zaf looked at the cat carrier in his hands. "I'm not taking Boudicca home."

"What else are you going to do?" said Newton. "You can't just abandon her."

"Have you seen my flat? I mean, for one, it's Alexsei's flat, not mine. And it's, like, actually nice. Boudicca would destroy it."

"Fine," sighed Diana. "Swap."

She passed him the carrier bag of old and mostly useless paperwork she'd picked up from the studio and took Boudicca's cat carrier from him. The fearsome moggy spat and threw herself against the side.

"Hang on," he said. "You've got no room in that place you share with your mum."

"Good job I know people then," she said. "Now." She turned around. "Let's head to the Redhouse Hotel and avail ourselves of their cocktail bar."

"Bit pricey in there," Newton pointed out.

"Tonight we drown our sorrows. I'm buying." She led the way down the road.

"Newton's probably on the ginger beers. It'll be a cheap round," Zaf muttered.

He returned home several hours later to the smell of fried food.

"Just in time," called Alexsei from the kitchen.

"Sorry I'm late," Zaf called back. "A few commiserative work drinks. Ginger beer two nights in a row."

He went through to the kitchen, where Alexsei was busy pushing sizzling peppers and beansprouts and other things around in a wok. Zaf stood behind Alexsei and put a kiss on his boyfriend's cheek.

"Smells good."

"I'm experimenting."

"Oh, dear."

Alexsei had been doing a lot of experimenting in the kitchen of late. Having cut all financial ties and some emotional ties with his father, Alexsei had become a young man with plenty of cash reserves and no real aims in life. The word he and Zaf sometimes used was 'dilettante'. Alexsei played some music and did some charity volunteering, but had yet to find something he could honestly call work.

At least the cooking benefitted them both. And it gave Alexsei a chance to exercise a creative side that didn't always come naturally.

"Is it ready to eat?" Zaf asked.

"I don't know. How burned should peppers be when you stir fry them?"

"I think it's probably ready."

Zaf put out plates and Alexsei served up. Before Zaf could take the food to the table, Alexsei had wrapped him in a hug, hands against the small of Zaf's back.

Zaf laughed. "What's this? We have to eat before your burned experiment goes cold."

"I'm offering you solace," said Alexsei. "You've lost your job, right?"

Zaf tensed. He'd lost his job. Chartwell and Crouch had closed its doors, probably for the very last time.

"I'll find something," he said.

Alexsei kissed him. "You don't have to hurry."

"I could just be a kept man? No. I would drive you insane."

"I do love you."

"Love's got nothing to do with it." Zaf returned the kiss, then extricated himself and took their dinners to the table by the patio doors.

Alexsei's apartment was on the fourth floor of a wharf development in Wapping. The patio doors led onto a balcony that looked out over the Thames, with stunning views of Tower Bridge and the Shard.

"Even the best of relationships can turn sour," said Zaf. "I've just heard the sorry saga of how Diana and Ariadne managed to ruin a perfectly good friendship while members of a popular pop band. It's a complicated tale."

"Does it need diagrams?" asked Alexsei.

Zaf speared a piece of pepper. It was burned, but it was also fried in chilli oil and tasted delicious.

"Let's see," he said. "Let me give you the short version."

Chapter Forty-Eight

Alexsei pulled his chair closer to the table and sipped a glass of wine. "I'm ready to take notes."

"Diana and Ariadne were best friends who joined a band with Morris and Pascal and Ken," said Zaf.

"This already sounds like the beginning of a riddle."

"Together they made beautiful music. Or at least, pleasant little electronic New Wave tunes that the kids jumped around to. Diana and Ariadne rented a flat together off Mr George Harrison of Beatles fame. And then Ariadne fell in love with Pascal. They all loved to party, but Pascal loved to party too much."

"As you've mentioned before." Alexsei swallowed some rice.

"The drinking got worse and so did the records. Quality went down and cracks began to appear. Ariadne took Pascal to LA to get help."

"This is news to me."

"Only found out about it today," said Zaf. "What Diana didn't know was that both of them were using that opportunity to try to get a fresh record deal for them, just the two of them, as a partnership."

"Oh."

"Diana had blamed Ariadne for it, but it wasn't just her. By this point, Diana was the sole occupant of the flat. Ariadne had her man. Meanwhile, Morris had been investing his money wisely and, when times were lean for the others, bought out their rights to the ElectraBeat music catalogue."

"See? Bands always fall out over money."

"Morris bought into the tour guide business and employed Diana. Ariadne went off to work for ACE Tours. Pascal was very slowly getting his life back together. Ken, I think, just carried on doing music work here and there. He seems genuinely happy with the life he's led."

Alexsei prodded his food in the manner of a man who wasn't entirely enamoured with his own creation. "And now most of them aren't talking to each other," he said.

"Um, yeah. Sort of." Zaf thought about it. "Ariadne isn't talking to Pascal because Pascal was a drunk who kind of wasted a chunk of her life for her. Diana wasn't talking to Ariadne because she thought Ariadne was the one who engineered the band split. Maybe Ariadne isn't talking to Morris because he was the only one who seemed to make a profit out of the band, especially when one of their tunes got sampled for a hit hip-hop record not long after the rest of them had sold him their rights."

"I'd be miffed if someone took all the profits from my recording career," said Alexsei.

"And then Ariadne wasn't talking to Diana because Diana was the shoulder Pascal cried on once he'd turned his life around. By the way, I think Diana and Pascal might have a bit of a thing for each other."

Alexsei wagged his fork at Zaf warningly. "You thought that last time because you sneakily read Diana's diaries and jumped to the wrong conclusions."

Zaf shrugged. "I think Pascal nearly dying has possibly made the two of them realise they should seek some happiness while they can."

"You're just a romantic." Alexsei squeezed Zaf's hand across the table. "And who is Ken not talking to?"

Zaf smiled. "Ken's happy to talk to anyone. He doesn't seem to bear any grudges at all."

"We should all be more like Ken," said Alexsei, nodding.

"Absolutely." Zaf chewed a mouthful. "Mmmm. Speaking of things dredged up from the past, we found some documents at the studio. Thought you might like to look."

"Me?"

Zaf jumped up to get the carrier bag of papers. "There's Diana's original contract for the flat in Ecclestone Square. You were the landlord so—"

"*Were* is very much the operative word there, Zaf. I've washed my hands of the place and my father."

"You do need to start talking to him again."

Alexsei was unconvinced. "He's the one who needs to build the bridges."

"He's the old man who, when he dies, you will regret not loving better."

"OK. When I said we should all be more like Ken, I didn't mean you should start bullying me into making things up with my dad." Alexsei washed down the last of his food with a swig of wine and looked at the document he'd been given. "Well, this isn't Diana's tenancy contract."

"No, that's the original one. The actual original with George Harrison's actual signature on the bottom as landlord."

Alexsei flicked through the yellow papers. "I know my dad's company had to set up a mirror agreement with Diana when they bought the property. Ridiculously low rent." He'd found the last page. "Wow. George Harrison's signature. Bet that's worth a few quid. But... this isn't Diana's signature."

"Oh, not you too."

Diana had been finally evicted from her home because of a slip of the pen. Diana was her middle name, not her first name. Kamran Dadashov's legal team had managed to invalidate her tenancy agreement based on a discrepancy between the two sets of names.

"No, I mean it's not Diana's name at all," Alexsei pointed out.

He showed Zaf.

"Oh, yes. That," said Zaf. "Ariadne signed the agreement and then sub-let to Diana. I think that's what happened. If anything, the agreement your dad set up should probably have been with Ariadne."

"Yeah, funny that," said Alexsei. "Diana didn't want to sign or something?"

"Maybe afraid of the commitment. You know, putting your name to some property, tying yourself to it. It's a scary step."

Alexsei laughed.

"What?" said Zaf.

"Scared of commitment, says the man who is happy to let me put my name to a piece of property that you live in."

Zaf frowned. "You want me to pay rent?"

"No," said Alexsei.

"I can!"

"No you can't, and that's not what I meant," said Alexsei, grinning. "But maybe... maybe you won't be afraid of making a commitment with me one day."

Zaf eyed him warily. "Are you proposing?"

Alexsei blinked. "Um. No. I, er, was actually wondering if we should get a dog or something."

"Ah," said Zaf, suddenly nervous. "If it helps, I came very close to bringing a cat home with me tonight."

"Cats are nice too," said Alexsei.

"No. Not this one."

Chapter Forty-Nine

The next two weeks passed in a whirl of activity.

Diana might have been in her sixties, but she'd been busy her whole life and had no intention of slowing down. Her energies had to be diverted somewhere.

She applied for three jobs: Curator for the Florence Nightingale Museum at St Thomas Hospital, Events Co-ordinator for the Festival Hall on the South Bank, and Community Engagement Officer with an education charity in Walthamstow. Off the applications went, but by the time the fortnight was over, no replies had come back.

She met up with Zaf and Newton regularly for support and encouragement. She'd taken over an empty bedsit near Russell Square, a place that was far too noisy with the sound of the tube line below for a human to live in, but which suited Boudicca perfectly. The place belonged to a friend of a friend of Chaz, and she was trying not to think too much about that.

Her former colleagues came round to the flat she now thought of as Boudicca's. Diana was all for contacting Battersea Dogs Home (who didn't just rehome dogs) but Newton resisted. Neither of them had found a new job. It didn't look like Zaf had actually started looking. Diana had sent off a number of e-mails to Rita de la Cruz enquiring about redundancy pay. Rita had replied, assuring her that there would be such a thing, but no details were included.

And also during those two weeks, she met with Pascal Palmer for three delightful lunch dates. Pascal was mostly recovered from his injury. There was a dark brown scabby line running through his fine white hair, and there would probably be a permanent scar, but both his general health and his mood seemed very much back to normal. They spoke of the old days, but also of future plans. Pascal was contemplating going on a cruise around the Mediterranean and was clearly building up to inviting her along. The notion did have a certain appeal.

It was during their third meal out that Diana received a message from Chaz, inviting her to a preview of the as-yet-unnamed cat album at the studios on Abbey Road on the coming Friday. She responded saying that she would be delighted to be there, even though her appreciation of cat-music might be somewhat limited.

She asked Pascal to join her, for his own entertainment and as moral support.

"I wouldn't want to let you out of my sight," he said.

A follow up message added that Ken 'insisted' the cat stars came along to the preview. It was all bonkers, but very much in keeping with the tone of the project.

On the day of the preview, Zaf, Alexsei and Newton came over to Russell Square with a cat carrier and protective clothing to help round up Boudicca. The fiery-tempered cat had made herself very much at home in the abandoned bedsit. At the start of her incarceration, Newton had set up a camera in the living room so he could keep an eye on her welfare. She seemed to spend most of her days in the living room window communicating loudly with the traffic that went by outside. She still did a good impression of the tube trains, but now she had added credible imitations of both throaty heavy good vehicles and zippy scooters.

The taxi dropped them off outside the Grove End Studio in the early light evening. A pleasantly balmy air hung over St John's Wood. It was an evening made for companionship and gentle conviviality.

Chaz Chase was at the door, wearing a tuxedo and bowtie.

"I didn't realise this was a red carpet event," said Diana. "I would have dressed up."

"You shine like a diamond regardless, love," said Chaz, taking both of her hands in greeting. "It's a swanky do tonight. Last chance to splash the cash on this project and put in some extra tax-deductible expenses."

"You're only going to be able to claim back expenses on any actual income this album makes," she pointed out.

"Good job I took out some actual insurance, then. Either way I'm a winner."

Chaz had handshakes for Alexsei, Zaf and Newton and an amused grin for the two cats in their carriers. There was already a crowd in Studio One, which had been set out with concert seating. Big Ernie was in conversation with Tom Griffin and Ariadne, who wore a sparkling floor-length dress. Ken Ferrari, still sporting his arm sling, had added a bowtie to one of his painfully bright shirts. He was grinning uncontrollably while he chatted to Pascal. By contrast, the sound engineer Tracy still wore a permanent scowl.

"Is that woman ever happy?" asked Zaf.

"Maybe she just hides it well," said Diana.

Ariadne approached them, glass of fizz in hand. She had eyes only for the cat in Zaf's carrier.

"How has this wonderful girl been?" she cooed. "I've missed her so much."

"Really?" said Zaf. "Perhaps you'd like to help me get her into her, er, private listening booth."

Zaf carried Boudicca over to the booth that had been set up as Boudicca's prison-cum-play-pen, and Ariadne gladly assisted. Zaf had insisted that Alexsei come along to see the luxury that had been provided for the feral moggy.

"No such confinement for you, mate," Newton said to Gus, and setting his carrier on the floor, let him out into the main studio. Newton followed his friend at a discreet distance, engaging people in chit-chat about Gus, the singing star, as though he was the tabby cat's PR representative.

Pascal, in a freshly-pressed linen suit, came over to Diana and placed a warm kiss on her cheek.

"This is a strange event," he said with a smile.

"A cat concert? Yes."

"That, true. But also the fact that... Have you not noticed that this is almost entirely the same crowd who were here on the night your manager chap fell to his death?"

"It had crossed my mind," she said. "And, yes, it's chilling in its own way. It's like a little part of me expects him to come walking in at any moment. And then make some stupid crass statement about his next brilliant business plan."

"Never a sensible chap, was he?"

"Not at all," agreed Diana. "But it's still a tragedy." She reached up and ran her fingers close to the scar on Pascal's head. "Not all hurts can be undone."

"We can only find our own personal peace with things. The police no further with the investigation?"

She waved her hand around at the other people in the room. "There's half a dozen motives in the room right here," she said.

"You think one of them did it?"

"Anyone here could have done it, just about, but no one was really in the right place at the right time. Between the lack of forensics and your foggy recollection of the attack I think the police will end up settling for the idea that Paul threw himself off the fire escape. Either that, or they'll just have to accept it was some mysterious unknown assailant."

Pascal grunted. "Some mysteries must remain unsolved."

Chapter Fifty

"Ladies and gentlemen," called Chaz, taking to a microphone at the centre of the studio. "Please take your seats for the performance."

Pascal fetched a glass of fizz for Diana and an orange juice for himself.

"Cheap caterer's Cava," he pointed out to her. "The orange juice is better, however you look at it."

They took seats side by side. Zaf and Alexsei took the seats beside them.

"I must remember to have a word with you later," Alexsei said to Diana.

"Oh?" she said.

"A legal matter that might be of interest to you. It hinges somewhat on your relationship with Ariadne Webb."

Pascal laughed at that. "Can anyone have a relationship with that woman?"

Two rows in front, Ariadne seemed to stiffen in her seat, but did not turn round, pretending not to hear.

Diana would have asked Alexsei more about what this legal

matter might be, but Chaz now had everyone seated and was ready to talk.

"Right," said Chaz. "For those who 'aven't been here before, welcome to the new and improved Grove End Studios. For those who 'ave, I hope we can 'ave a happier evening than the last time we were all here."

There were some solemn nods.

"Ken's proper excited about the material that we laid down," said Chaz. "I mean, those cats can make a decent sound, but after Ken and Tracy get to work, it's summat else. We might 'ave a hit on our 'ands, ladies and gents."

There was gentle laughter.

"But you don't wanna hear me talking about it," said Chaz. "You wanna hear from the producer himself, who will be introducing you to some selected excerpts of his 'masterpiece'."

There was polite applause for Ken as he took the microphone.

"Friends. Friends of all stripe, creed and colour, this has been a labour of love," he said. "The world has made music for humans for thousands of years. The world has made music for cats only in recent, more enlightened times. But only now have we finally recorded music that is made *by* humans and cats and *for* humans and cats."

"This is different," Alexsei whispered to Zaf.

"Let's wait and see," Zaf whispered back. Diana gave him a nudge.

"Tracy, if you're ready," said Ken, waving to the control room. "We will start with the opening movement *Lament for the Midnight Mice*."

Pascal just about concealed a laugh at the pompous title of the track. And then the music started.

It began with violins, and then, over them, the sound of the cat singing. It was Boudicca's voice, clearly Boudicca. Diana listened as the sound of Boudicca's unearthly yowl was joined by the swelling strings of an orchestra. Somehow, just somehow, the two melded together, harmonising. The cat's monotonous scream was the bass note on which the orchestral melody rested. It was rich and unusual, but surprisingly appealing. It put Diana in mind of a Bjork song, ethereal and unworldly but undoubtedly tuneful.

"Hear how its dark sad melody is filled with yearning?" said Ken, clutching at the air as if delivering a Shakespearean soliloquy.

Everyone listened in silence. Gus stood up on a chair, his head twitching from side to side as though he couldn't work out where the soulful cat was singing from. In the window of her private booth, Boudicca seemed equally mystified.

"They think there's another cat in here," Zaf whispered.

"A singing cat," agreed Diana.

The song faded and there was applause. Diana was surprised: the thing had actually worked.

"It's amazing how they brought the tune right out of the cat," Tom Griffin said to Ariadne in the rows in front.

"Man's a genius," replied Ariadne. "I helped train the cat, you know."

"Now, this is one of Gus's tracks, that we're calling *Morning Sunshine Patrol*," said Ken as he gestured to Tracy to play the next one.

Gus's jaunty tune was very different. HIs vocals had been layered into a complex and tuneful composition that reminded Diana of Keith West's *Excerpt from a Teenage Opera* with its sense of busy drama. Again, somehow, through sheer wizardry, the cat sounds and the music worked together with such tuneful intricacy that it wasn't a stretch to believe Gus had been singing from a score sheet.

Chaz leaned over the back of Diana's chair and quietly asked, "Is this good? Is this actually good?"

"You know what, I think it is," she replied, mystified.

"Oh, this is not what I asked for," he fumed. "People are actually gonna listen to this, aren't they?"

"In their millions," added Pascal wryly.

"I have to admit I was uncertain," said Diana, "but I should never have doubted Ken. He recognises the nuggets of pure gold in performers."

"Always has done, I reckon," said Pascal. "Even back in the day, he was always an enabler. The glue that held us together when we were already coming apart."

Diana smiled. "It's good to hear that he still has his superpowers."

Ariadne turned in her seat to face them. "He just takes what's already there and weaves a recording around it and turns it into something new."

"Not a hit record," said Chaz, irritated. "I don't need a hit record on my hands."

Diana noticed Alexsei frowning.

"Insurance scam," Zaf whispered. "Turning a profit from a disaster."

And as the song ended and the applause started, Diana felt something shift inside her.

The truth. She knew the truth.

She knew who had killed Paul Kensington and attacked Pascal Palmer.

Chapter Fifty-One

Diana lurched to her feet.

Zaf looked at her. "Are you OK?"

She looked down at him with a frown.

"Are you unwell, my dear?" asked Pascal.

Diana said nothing. She seemed unable to speak.

"If you're about to begin a spontaneous standing ovation then I won't say no," joked Ken from the microphone stand.

Diana patted Zaf's arm as she moved along the row of chairs. "We need to call the police," she said.

"What's happened?" asked Tom Griffin.

"I know who did it," muttered Diana.

"Did what?" asked Newton.

"All of it," she said. "All of it. The ticket fraud, Pascal's injury, Paul's death, the attempt to run me over right outside this studio."

Ernie turned to her. "Really?"

Diana nodded. Her skin was pale.

"Oh, dearie me," said Ariadne. "She's having one of her moments."

"I am not having a 'moment'," Diana insisted. "I know and... yes! Of course! That explains the window!"

"What window?" asked Chaz.

Zaf exchanged a look with Alexsei, who shrugged. He hoped Diana was OK. Should he follow her?

"The broken window next to the fire exit," Diana said. "The one the attacker went out of."

She stepped away from the seated audience, looking for space. "It's like Paul is dead."

"We know Paul's dead," said Newton.

"No, not Paul is dead. The conspiracy theory 'Paul is dead'. It's like that. Sort of."

"Diana, we've seen this act before." Ariadne rose to her feet and addressed the group. "My dear old friend has a penchant for making accusations of murder at public gatherings. Last time, if I recall rightly, it was at a graduation ceremony at St Paul's." She rolled her eyes. "The scene she caused."

Zaf had seen Diana do this many times now. He'd been involved. She hadn't always got it right, at least not at first. But she understood people. And her memory, her attention to detail...

"If Diana knows something then let her speak," he said. "Chaz, can you call the police?"

Chaz looked at Zaf. He shook his head.

"I'll call the police," said Newton.

Chaz drew himself up. "I'd rather you didn't, sunshine."

"Chaz, you have nothing to fear," said Diana.

Unless the fraud squad decided to show an interest in Chaz's business accounting, thought Zaf. It was clear that Chaz had planned the cat album as some tax-dodging money-laundering ruse.

"Oh, so Chaz isn't your number one suspect?" said

Ariadne. "That bitter and horrible review would have been enough to make anyone want to bash Pascal's brains in."

"I was only writing the truth," said Pascal.

Chaz grunted. "A fairly mean-spirited stab at the truth, mate."

"And I doubt it made any difference to the numbers of people coming through your door."

Chaz gave an indifferent shrug. "Still the kind of language that might get an old boy slapped round the chops if he came in my boozer."

"Hear that?" said Ariadne to Diana. "Are you going to be pointing your finger at Chaz?"

Diana shook her head. "Chaz had reason to dislike Pascal, but he's not the only one."

"That's true," said Pascal. "Ready to put your hands up and admit you were the one who clobbered me, Ariadne dear?"

"I think we two have punished each other enough," she said. "Not one of us in the band hasn't wished all the others dead at some point. That's showbiz, honey."

"I don't think I wished anyone dead," said Ken.

"Well, you're different, Ken-doll," replied Ariadne.

"Different how?" he asked.

Ariadne puffed out her cheeks and gestured at him: his lurid shirt, his silly dickie bow, his bulky arm sling.

"However," said Diana, "crucially, Ken did tell Pascal about the demo tapes left up in Studio Three. Without that fact, there would have been no reason for Pascal to be up there."

"Are you saying I'm responsible?" said Ken, aghast. "I didn't mean to..."

"No one's going to lay any blame at your door simply for

telling Pascal there might be something of interest in that room—"

"Unless he said it to lure Pascal there," put in Tracy.

"Tracy!" said Ken.

The sound engineer shrugged. "I'm just saying. X follows Y. Maybe you did want him up there."

"I'm your colleague, Tracy! Why would you say such things?"

"It would have been a struggle for Ken to have attacked Pascal," said Diana. "If we accept the evidence of our senses, then at the very moment Pascal was being attacked, Ken was breaking his shoulder in his attempt to get into that room."

"The evidence of our senses?" said Ariadne.

Diana nodded. "It's all about time, and what we saw and heard. There are any number of us here who could just about have hit Pascal and then pushed Paul and then got to another place so they could act all innocent."

"So, you're saying someone in this room *did* do it?" said Ernie.

"Definitely," Diana replied. "Pascal asked me as we came in if I thought one of you lot did it and that's where my true suspicions have lain since the very beginning. Forget all those silly notions about a surprised burglar. The killer meticulously planned this crime. It's been sufficiently well thought out that I was quite stumped until now. All us here who did not have any part in it, know that we did not have any part in it, but most of you would find it hard to vouch for each other and find anyone else to vouch for you."

"Well, I was with you and Ken," said Tom, "so everyone knows I didn't do it."

"True," said Diana. "But it's still conceivable that you

wished Paul harm. The sooner he was out of the way, the sooner you could snap up any assets at Chartwell and Crouch."

"That's not how I operate," said Tom. "And it's definitely not part of the ACE Tours ethos."

"And surely Pascal was the target," said Ernie. "The attacker hit Pascal, jumped out the window, pushed that Paul character off the stairs and then ran off."

"Paul makes a more convincing victim," said Zaf, then realised how odd that sounded.

"He does," said Diana. "Paul – I'm very sorry to say – was a much disliked man, and yes, I am absolutely certain that he was the murderer's intended victim."

"So, who would want to kill him?" said Ken.

Diana gestured across the whole group as though she could pick any one of them.

"Newton Crombie," she said.

Chapter Fifty-Two

"M e?" squeaked Newton.

"You did say the sooner he dies, the better," said Diana.

"A figure of speech!"

"Of course," Diana replied. "*I* could have wished him dead. His business practices were the antithesis of what good tour guiding should be. Zaf too, I suppose, might have cause to wish violence on the man who was destroying his livelihood."

"I didn't..." Zaf began, his heart leaping in his chest.

"No, of course you didn't," said Diana.

Alexsei's hand gripped Zaf's. "I thought that was about to get too exciting for a moment there," he whispered.

"It is plain to me," said Diana, "that the person who killed Paul is the same person who swindled all those poor tour guide customers out of their money. It was someone who had been intimately familiar with the people at Chartwell and Crouch for many years. You were still in school when that first crime was committed."

She moved towards the microphone. Gus padded across the floor to sit at her feet.

"I don't think there is a single one of us here," she said, scanning the group, "who is not aware that Chartwell and Crouch customers were swindled out of a vast amount of money by a bogus ticket website, money that was never recovered. Our friend and former bandmate, Morris Walker, is currently in Wandsworth jail, still serving a lengthy sentence for that crime. And Morris is innocent."

"Come now," said Ernie. "Diana, you've been suckered in by a jailbird's whiny pleas of innocence."

"No, it's true," said Zaf, standing to address Ernie. "At the time Morris was allegedly withdrawing the cash from the bank, he claimed he was at a café and met this woman and her dog, Marengo. I saw the dog some weeks back. And Diana tracked down the woman. It all fits together."

"So, he had an accomplice," said Pascal.

"I remember you suggesting that when I told you about Marengo," said Diana. "Morris and Paul. Working together. That makes sense in some ways."

"See?" said Ernie.

"A week or so before he died, Paul Kensington showed me a key to a locker off Baker Street. When the police came to the depot, they found the key and I saw them open the locker. But it was empty."

"There was that money on Paul's body," said Tom Griffin, pointing with excitement at the memory.

"The John Houblon fifty pound notes," agreed Zaf. "They're not legal tender now but they were when the cash was taken out of the bank. And when the auditor woman came to shut us down—"

"A sad, sad day," said Newton.

"We found a huge bag of cash, the same cash, in Newton's secret attic workshop."

A dozen heads swivelled to look at Newton.

"Not that Newton put it there," Zaf added hurriedly.

"But Paul did," said Diana. "He put the cash there. And he was planning to spend it. A number of us heard him on that final day going on about some new 'high level funding' he'd just come into. He was planning on using that money."

"So Morris hired someone to kill Paul," suggested Pascal. "To stop him spending the loot while Morris was still locked up."

"But Paul wasn't in league with Morris," said Diana. "He couldn't have been. I came into the office that morning while I was on the phone, and Paul literally asked me if I knew what the key was for. He didn't know. No. The person who had put the money in the locker had done it a long time ago and then left the key in the depot office."

"Morris again," said Pascal.

"Or someone who wanted everyone to think Morris had stolen the money. Morris was innocent and, for a while, I was the only person who had all the pieces of evidence to prove his alibi was true. I think that's why someone tried to run me over."

"I still can't believe that," said Chaz. "Bleedin' scandalous."

"I believe Paul died because he found that money," said Diana. "More specifically, I think he died because he found that money and didn't take it to the police. If Morris is innocent, which he is, then the reason that key was in the office was as evidence planted to further damn our former bandmember."

"Why try to frame him now when he's already serving time?" asked Ariadne. "I'm sorry, Diana, but this doesn't add up." She stood and went to fetch herself another glass of fizz.

"Get me an orange juice," Pascal called after her.

"Get one yourself," she called back.

"Ariadne," said Diana, "it makes sense if the key had just been sat there, all those years, waiting to be found."

As Pascal got up to get a juice, Ariadne said, "I don't see how you're going to accuse anyone of this murder. You say I could have done it, out of hatred for Pascal, which is something I still have?"

"Thank you," said Pascal, standing at the table by the door.

"But apparently I didn't. You say Chaz could have done it because of Pascal's vile and poisonous reviews."

Pascal narrowed his eyes at Ariadne. "Thank you again, my dear."

"But apparently, he didn't," Ariadne said. "Tom might have wanted Paul out of the way. Newton hated him because he's in love with his old buses."

"I... I..." Newton rose to his feet, beginning to protest, then sat down again with a nod. "It's true," he said. "I do love them."

Ariadne turned to Diana. "You and Zaf might have harboured equal hatred, but of course you didn't kill Paul because you're the great detectives. Sherlock Holmes and Doctor Watson."

"Am I Watson?" Zaf asked Alexsei.

"You say that any of us could have done it, but then say none of us did."

"Is it me?" asked Alexsei, planting a splayed hand on his own chest. "Are you going to accuse me?"

"Well, don't look at me," said Tracy Chen. "I didn't even know the dead dude."

Zaf did a count of the people in the room.

"Ernie?" he suggested when he'd run out of people.

"Watch your mouth, lad," said Big Ernie.

"If you will just permit me to explain," said Diana, hands

raised. "It was Ariadne who finally made me see it. Five minutes ago. We were talking about Ken's work on the recording and she said, 'he just takes what's already there in and weaves a recording around it'."

"So?" said Ariadne.

"That's how it was done," said Diana. "A blending of what was happening and what had never really happened at all. It is, truly, like the Paul is dead conspiracy. People heard John Lennon saying what they thought was 'I buried Paul' embedded in a record or listened to certain key lyrics and they took that audio information as proof that the man they loved had come to an unpleasant end."

"But he hadn't," said Zaf.

"But he hadn't," repeated Diana.

Alexsei frowned. "Paul Kensington wasn't dead?"

Diana tutted. "No. Paul Kensington was dead. Different Paul. But our killer misled us all. It's like Morris. He's getting the lads in prison to do a production of 'Oliver!'."

"Oh, that's nice," said Ken.

"And because they might not want to perform live, he's got them miming to a recording of themselves. Just like he did in the old days of ElectraBeat. Record his vocals first so he could be doing something else while we sang along with him."

"And this has got something to do with the murder, has it?" asked Ken.

"Absolutely. And it's absolutely to do with the fact that Chaz got you in the other week to check the studios."

Diana looked round the room. Zaf saw an expression of puzzlement cloud her face.

"Blast," she whispered to herself. "I'm sorry."

"What is it?" said Zaf.

"I think she's run out of steam," said Ariadne.

"I'm sorry," Diana said again. "If you'll all excuse me..."

She skirted around the chairs and went out the door.

"Does she do this murder scene thing often?" asked Tom Griffin.

"Surprisingly frequently," said Ariadne. "I think if we're having a break, I might go check on my dear Boudicca."

Newton looked about.

"Has Gus wandered off again?" Alexsei asked him.

Zaf looked about the room, trying to fathom why Diana had left so suddenly. Had the killer slipped out unnoticed?

He did a head count of all the possible suspects and impossible suspects. Tom, Ariadne, Newton, Chaz, Ernie, Ken, Tracy, Alexsei and himself – all were here.

Chapter Fifty-Three

Diana climbed the stairs to the second floor. She moved quietly and listened out.

There was a small scrabbling sound. She'd been right to come up instead of going out into the street.

She took out her phone and dialled a number.

The door to Studio Three was slightly ajar. She pushed it open and looked through into the control room of the small studio.

"You slipped away stealthily," she said.

Pascal Palmer looked up from the control desk. The tight, fraught expression on his face was briefly replaced by an automatic smile.

"Ah." He picked up a small black object.

"A memory card," said Diana. "So much easier than the bulky tapes back in our day."

"I'm just tidying up here," he told her. "How's things going downstairs?"

"I was just getting to the good part," she replied. "The bit where I tell everybody that you killed Paul Kensington."

"Me?" said Pascal. Another smile.

"Yes," she said, feeling her chest flutter. "You stole the Chartwell and Crouch money and you killed Paul Kensington."

"Um, no. I don't think so. I was unconscious on the floor over there at the moment Paul fell to his death. In fact, I'm starting to think it was probably Paul who hit me. Yes. That makes sense."

"Stop, Pascal," said Diana. "Don't make me do it."

"I'm not making you do anything."

A bitter laugh brewed inside her. "Oh, you're making me do many things, Pascal. Consider how I must feel right now, after the moments we've shared these last weeks, even talk of travelling together, knowing that it was you – *you* – who tried to kill me on that zebra crossing."

"I was in hospital when that happened."

She shook her head. "You were being discharged that day. Ariadne mentioned it, but I didn't twig at the time. She's a smart cookie, really. I should have more respect for her."

"You're more alike than either of you is willing to admit."

Diana cocked her head. "You killed Paul and tried to kill me. Do you really want me to tell you how you did it?"

His smile changed. There was resignation in it, and a certain cold self-satisfaction.

"Please. I'm sure it's fascinating."

She stood at the spot where Pascal had fallen. The fading blood stain was still there on the wood floor.

"If I just step back through what happened, it's obvious it could only have been you. Paul Kensington, greedy and blinkered though he might be, was an innocent fool in all this. I was in the office when he found the locker key. He asked me if I knew what it was. I recall now that I was on the phone to you at the time. You literally heard him mention the key and describe it. You knew it well. You'd put the money in the locker and left the key in what was then Morris's office for the police to find. Except they didn't. Not for a decade."

"A bit remiss of them, I'd say."

She nodded. "Paul went and fetched the money some days later. I wonder if you were hovering outside, watching, waiting, assuming that any decent person would then take this haul of cash to the police. No, not stupid Paul. He thought he could use it to plot his next money-wasting scheme. Did you try to approach him? Push him towards turning the money in?"

Pascal pulled a face and shrugged.

"But, no," said Diana. "He wasn't going to do that. You'd spent years building a plot to frame Morris for a massive ticket fraud, and even though Morris was already in jail, you still had one last twist of the knife to deliver with the evidence of the loot. Paul hid the money at work and that final piece of your wonderful crime was never going to slot into place."

"If you say so."

"So you decided to kill Paul. You knew he was going to be invited to the studio launch party. You had already been there. You helped Ken with some technical checks. Chaz told me that the night of the launch. You had time in the studio to prepare. You possibly made your recording here."

"Doing it in situ seemed best," said Pascal, looking at the tiny memory card in his hand. "The acoustics would match."

"You recorded a violent encounter between yourself and an attacker. You played both of the voices. The actual words were unimportant. All you needed were the voices and some rough noises to make it sound like you were in here the entire time."

"I think I did a good job."

"You did. On the evening of the party, you came up here because 'Ken had told you about some old demo tapes'. That was your excuse. And then, once up here, you phoned Paul Kensington from that telephone there." She pointed at the phone in the control room. "Now, everyone who's worked here knows there's no signal in the building, and you knew Paul was on the fire escape because the signal suddenly improved. You would even have heard him go by on the metal steps. And then you played your recording."

He nodded.

"Ariadne and I played some, er – what were they called? – Gorgeous Alien Dolls in here. Those speakers are loud and clear. You can hear them downstairs. A recording of you shouting and fighting would be picked up a floor down, or even further. And when you heard us coming up the stairs, trying to open the door to reach you, you simply stepped out of the fire exit there and pushed Paul Kensington to his death." She felt sadness pull at her. "Did he say anything when you came out to kill him?"

Pascal shook his head. "He was smiling. He didn't suspect a thing. He was... he was surprisingly light. Like a child, almost."

Diana felt her mouth twist in anguish.

"You are an evil man, aren't you?"

"We all do what we have to."

She forced calm upon herself. "And then you came back in here. Via the door again. The smashed window was a curious thing which really didn't make sense. Why would your attacker smash their way out of the window when they could use the door? But you wanted the smashed window to add that point of realism. The recording and reality blurred together."

"Hokey, I know," said Pascal. "I think it worked."

"And then you came over here and, I suppose, you head-butted the instrument case with all your might."

"A little too much might," he said. "Nearly did myself in for real."

"Shame you didn't."

"You and I could have been happy, you know," he said, his voice harsh. "Golden years, spent together. As friends or more. We could have been happy. And now what? You, jobless, homeless, loveless. And I suppose I need to make alternative plans."

He stepped backwards, turned and went to the fire exit. He stepped out onto the metal stairs.

If she thought he was going to make his way down and escape, she was wrong. He went to the turn of the stairs and made his way up to the roof.

She followed.

There was a fresh breeze moving across the rooftops of London. St John's was a mosaic of square houses, elegant apartment blocks and thick green trees. Diana stepped onto the roof. Pascal stood, arms outstretched, taking deep breaths.

"You know you made an admission of sorts when I visited you in hospital," she said.

"Ah, that," said Pascal. "My mouth ran away with itself there. 'Gave *myself* a fearsome whack on the head' or something of that ilk. Yes. I was kicking myself afterwards. I think that anger was part of what drove me to get my car and head over here."

"That and the fact that I had told you what I knew about Morris's alibi," she said.

"Yes, and that."

"But, no. Not that admission. I told you in the hospital that I wasn't the kind of person to hold onto anger and hatred, and you said I was a better person than you."

"Ah," he said.

"You really did hate Morris, didn't you?"

"Still do," he said, almost cheerily. "We poured a lifetime of creativity into ElectraBeat, and then, when we were at our lowest ebb, he took our portions of it for himself and made a fortune."

"We sold our rights to him."

"When they were worth a pittance! But when we got sampled for that hit record, did we see a single penny? No. That man had no sense of loyalty to his friends. Not to a single one of us! He put the boot in while we were at our lowest and then just lorded it over us forever after."

"I don't... I don't think I see it that way."

"Then you're an even bigger fool than Ken bloody Ferrari," he spat. "Morris Walker deserved everything that happened to him. What was it you said earlier? Not all hurts can be undone?"

"But we can find our own personal peace."

Somewhere there was shouting. It sounded like Zaf's voice. Was he on the fire escape? Was he looking for her?

Pascal put his hands in his pockets and walked towards the edge of the roof. He looked towards the sunset.

"You know what," he said, "I think I like things the way they are. Morris is in prison for a crime he clearly committed. The money has been found. The rest of us have the freedom to get on with our lives."

"They'll let you do that in prison," she said.

His look was reproachful. "No. I definitely like things the

way they are. You won't tell anyone. I won't tell anyone. Life will go on."

He held out a hand to her.

"You know, out of all the people I've met on this journey, I do think I liked you most of all."

Chapter Fifty-Four

As Zaf ran up the fire escape, he heard a cry and then something plummeted past him, faster than he could follow. It hit the ground three storeys below and did not move. He glanced down and then ran on, up to the roof.

Diana stood at the edge of the flat roof by the parapet lip. She had her arms wrapped around herself, a phone clutched in one hand.

Zaf went to her, took hold of her shaking shoulders and guided her back from the edge.

"Diana..."

She seemed to notice him for the first time then, and passed her phone to him. There was a call open. The caller ID said Clint Sugarbrook.

Zaf put it to his ear.

"Hello?"

"Zaf? Zaf Williams?" said the detective.

"I don't know what's happened here," Zaf told him.

"I heard enough," said Sugarbrook. "Could you please get

Miss Bakewell down from the roof. The police are on their way."

"Yes." He ended the call and shepherded Diana towards the stairs.

"Pascal..." he said. "What did...?"

"He was never going to go to prison," she said.

Once they were down, he guided her to the other guests back in Studio One.

"She OK?" asked Alexsei.

"Compared to what?" said Zaf.

Newton cradled Gus in his arms as though his cat needed protecting from the madness in this place. More surprisingly, Ariadne sat with Boudicca on her knee, caressing her softly and not having her eyes gouged out by the mad creature.

An ambulance was outside on Abbey Road within fifteen minutes, one minute later than the first police car. For reasons Zaf wasn't sure of, Chaz Chase started to have an argument with the police officers as soon as they entered.

Ernie stood by, rolled his eyes, and let Chaz have his moment.

Tom Griffin had decided that, in the face of yet another death at the studios, cups of tea were called for once again. Tracy Chen helped him bring the drinks through. Ken, limited to the use of one arm, carried the biscuits.

Paramedics and then scenes of crime officers went through the back to the grey alley where Pascal Palmer's body lay.

While they waited for the wheels of the police investigation to turn, Zaf, Diana and Newton sat together. Diana held a cup of tea but did not drink.

Tom Griffin came over, turned a chair around and sat before them.

"I really don't know if this is the right time or a welcome

distraction," he said, "but while the three of you are here, I wanted to tell you something. Ask you something."

"Yes?" said Diana, her voice flat.

"It's about Chartwell and Crouch and the building and the buses."

"You've got my buses, haven't you?" said Newton. Gus added a meow of complaint.

"I... I have," replied Tom. "I bought them all when they became available."

Newton gave a ragged sigh. "I've still got some spares and the original manuals. If you need them, if you promise to look after them..."

"Actually," said Tom, "I'm in negotiations to take over the ownership of the depot building at Chiltern Street."

"Really?" said Zaf. "ACE Tours is expanding?"

"It is," said Tom. "We're always looking to add something new that we haven't already got."

Zaf nodded. The big sharks came along and ate the little fish. It was the way of the world.

"Perhaps you have some jobs going?" said Diana, with sideways nods to Zaf and Newton. "I will write the most glowing references."

"Us work for ACE Tours?" said Newton. "Without Diana?"

"No," said Tom. "I'd like all of you to become part of the ACE Tours family. As you were."

"I don't know," said Newton. "Does that mean I'd drive those Urbis two-point-five DD Open Tops. I really—"

"As you were," said Tom. "You are the heart and soul of the company. Zaf can create a magical tour experience for his customers with very little financial investment. Newton lavishes care on those beautiful vintage buses. And Diana has tried valiantly to steer a rudderless ship, with her experience and determination. I am thrilled to welcome Chartwell and Crouch to my modest portfolio. I would very much appreciate it if you will sign up to help me deliver tours using those vintage buses from that depot over in Marylebone."

"Everything can go back to exactly what it was before?" said Zaf.

"Gus can stay at the depot?" said Newton.

"We'd have to discuss the practicalities, but yes," said Tom. "And of course there would be a pay adjustment."

"You're getting everything at knock down prices," said Newton.

Tom wrinkled his nose and pointed upwards. "A long-overdue pay adjustment."

"And the Londiniumarium?" asked Diana. "Paul's pet project?"

"We wouldn't touch it with a twelve-foot barge pole," said Tom. "I want you to do the things that you *should* be doing. Lay on the tours that your customers deserve."

"For real?" beamed Zaf.

"For real," said Tom.

Diana frowned. "I'm not sure. I assume this might mean Ariadne and me working together. She might have something to say on the matter."

"Actually," said Tom. "She was the one that suggested it. Or at least prodded me in that direction."

Zaf looked across to Ariadne, who stood behind Tom, stroking Boudicca like a James Bond villain caressing a long-haired puss and looking very pleased with herself.

"I think Diana and I need to spend more time together," she said.

"It's worth a shot," said Diana.

Newton shook his head. "How do you not get savaged by that creature?"

Ariadne smiled. "Boudicca has been misunderstood for a long time. She has the biggest personality you can imagine, and she does not suffer fools gladly."

"Wait," said Zaf, "are we the fools in that sentence?"

"Boudicca responds well to a certain amount of firmness, and delicious fish," said Ariadne, ignoring the question. "I have decided she will be coming home with me, where she can live in regal splendour on her own terms. She and I might perform duets from time to time, who knows? She enjoys singing, that much is clear."

"That makes a lot of sense," said Newton. "Boudicca likes you."

"She tolerates me," said Ariadne. "Make no mistake. But I can live with that."

DCI Sugarbrook entered Studio One.

"Right," he said to the confined guests and staff, "I will make this as brief as possible and then you can be on your way. We will need to take statements from you. Miss Bakewell, might I have a word?"

Diana passed her untouched tea to Zaf and went over to Sugarbrook. The detective raised an arm to guide her out of the room.

As Tom took himself off to fetch more teas for those who needed a fortifying brew, Alexsei came and sat down next to Zaf.

"Do I hear that things might be on a more even keel between Diana and Ariadne?" he asked.

"Wonders will never cease," said Newton. Gus miaowed.

"Oh, good," said Alexsei. "That make this legal matter all the more promising."

"You mentioned something about that before the cat concert started," said Zaf.

Alexsei nodded. "I checked with my own lawyers this morning—"

"Lawyers. Plural," Zaf said to Newton.

Alexsei smiled. "I do engage the services of lawyers, plural, yes. I had them look over that old tenancy agreement you found the other day."

"The George Harrison one?"

"Yes. George rented out the flat to Ariadne. He never rented it out to Diana. Technically, legally, Diana had been sub-letting it through Ariadne for at least two decades."

"Which means?"

"Diana had an agreement with my father's company. The one she signed with her common name, Diana, rather than her legal name, Patricia, and which Shivdler Legal subsequently declared to be null and void."

"Yes, we know," said Zaf.

"Well, that agreement shouldn't have existed in the first place. My father's company should have made a legal agreement with Ariadne, the actual tenant. They set up a contract with the wrong person."

Zaf was frowning. He felt he was on the cusp of understanding.

"So...?"

Alexsei gave a genial shrug. "I've discussed the facts with my lawyers – plural – and their conclusion is that my father's company has been renting out that property illegally for at least twenty years and would now be required to put it right, as stipulated in the agreement with Mr Harrison when he sold the property to my father."

Chapter Fifty-Five

Pascal Palmer's funeral was held at the City of London Cemetery in Aldersbrook.

Diana Bakewell, Ariadne Webb, Ken Ferrari and Morris Walker stood side by side at the grave as the priest read the words of committal. There were no eulogies from Pascal's ElectraBeat bandmates. No music, no songs. They had come to see him buried and paid such minimal respects as any human deserved.

Zaf and Alexsei, appropriately suited, stood further down the hill, among the statuary and headstones. Their role was to provide distant support and, when it was all over, Alexsei had a surprise to share with Diana.

Meanwhile, huddled together against the stiff breeze that blew through the cemetery, Alexsei flicked through pictures on his phone and showed them to Zaf.

"This one?"

"No."

"This one?"

"Weird teeth."

"This one?"

"What's the write-up say?"

"*Pipsqueak is a charming little chap who really wants to be part of the family. He wouldn't suit a family with children or other small pets as he can be quite energetic when excited. He is very fond of food and does steal things he can eat from surfaces and even out of the kitchen sink.*"

"Kitchen sink? How big is this thing?"

Alexsei double-checked. "He's a Great Dane." He put his hand up to his own chest to indicate the dog's height.

"He might be a flippin' amazing Dane," said Zaf. "That's a hard no. Pipsqueak? Really?"

Alexsei smiled and continued scrolling through the images from the dog rescue home.

"You two not joining the others graveside?" asked a voice.

Zaf turned to see DCI Sugarbrook, strolling along the cemetery path with a small terrier dog on a lead.

Zaf nodded at the grave further up the hill. "We got the feeling that this one was for close personal friends and enemies."

The bulky detective nodded. "Friends and enemies. Often the same people in my experience. If either of you two ever gets bumped off, I'll put a hundred quid on the other one having done it."

"Well, that is a lovely thought," said Alexsei. "And have you come to spread cheer all around the graveyard?"

Sugarbrook's cheek twitched. "There's something that draws me to the funerals of crooks I've either nicked or wanted to nick."

"Need to be doubly sure they're dead?" asked Zaf.

"Something like that."

The dog sniffed at Zaf's shoes. He knew this dog; he'd met

it when he and Diana had got caught up in the death of an art dealer on the Thames. The poor thing had been left inside a houseboat on the docks.

"This is JMW Turner, isn't it?" he asked.

"The world famous painter?" said Alexsei.

"The bane of my life," said Sugarbrook with a wry smile.

"Really?" Alexsei crouched to fuss the friendly terrier. JMW Turner's thickly furred brows and chin gave him the air of a grumpy old man, but he was an enthusiastic little fellow and delighted by the attention. "Oh, he's lovely."

"That he may be, young sir, but we simply don't have the time for him. I'm doing shift work and my other half has a big commute. Oh, the girls fell in love with him at first, but you know kids. The infatuations come hard and blow over in days. My advice: never get a dog because you think someone else wants it. Only let one of these mutts into your home if it's what you want."

"And you don't want?" said Zaf. He exchanged a glance with Alexsei.

"My hours aren't fair on the dog. And I think I'm more of a cat person. Give me a pet that can look after itself most of the time. I don't need an extra child in the house."

"Well, he is just the most handsome thing," said Alexsei, standing up.

Sugarbrook was looking at them, half-expectant. Zaf narrowed his eyes.

"I told Diana we were perhaps looking for a dog," he said.

"Is that so?" said Sugarbrook.

"And maybe she mentioned that to you too?" he added.

"I couldn't honestly recall..."

"And you knew we were going to be here today."

For a police officer, Sugarbrook was bad at hiding lies. His big rounded shoulders lifted in an amiable shrug.

"Maybe you'd like to take him for a turn around the cemetery," he suggested lightly.

"Oh, like a test drive?" said Alexsei.

"If you will," said Sugarbrook, offering them the lead.

Chapter Fifty-Six

The priest wiped the dirt from his hands as he walked away from Pascal's grave. The four mourners remained, looking down at the unfilled hole.

"You think you know someone for over forty years..." said Ariadne.

"We all harbour strange secrets and feelings," said Diana.

"Are we sharing our feelings now?" asked Ken.

"If you like."

Ken flexed his arm, evidently enjoying the freedom of no longer having to wear his shoulder sling.

"I think it's nice that we're all back together."

"All of us," said Diana, looking at the coffin. "In a manner of speaking."

"And just for a day," added Morris. He glanced over his shoulder. Standing a respectable twenty feet away were a pair of officers from Wandsworth prison. They seemed to be enjoying being out in the sunshine.

"How much longer are they keeping you locked up?" asked Ariadne.

"Hopefully only a few more weeks," said Morris. "I've been informed that the courts are fast-tracking the quashing of my conviction. I hear even the Home Secretary has got involved."

"Still," she said ruefully. "Those years of your life..."

"I will not be getting those years back," said Morris, "but I take solace from the fact that I have not let my spirits be destroyed and, equally importantly, I am due an absolutely colossal compensation payout for wrongful conviction. I shall be rich, and I have already decided how I want to spend the money."

"Do tell," said Ariadne.

Morris Walker had a cheeky grin on his face as he looked at each of them in turn. "I'd like to get the band back together."

"Hell, no," said Diana and Ariadne as one, then laughed.

"OK, we'll definitely think about it," said Diana.

"Yes," said Ariadne. "Yes... I've thought about it, and it's a terrible idea."

"I like it," said Ken.

Still smiling at the insane notion of the eighties band reforming in their sixties and seventies, they walked down to the waiting cars near the crematorium.

"So, we're going for a pint now, right?" suggested Morris. "Any funeral has to be followed by a wake."

"I'm afraid that's not part of the plan, Morris," said one of the prison guards.

"Really?" he said. "You know I'm going to be a free man soon. And this round's on me. I know a nice little boozer five minutes' drive from here."

The prison guards looked tempted.

Zaf and Alexsei approached. Alexsei had JMW Turner on a lead, which brought a smile to Diana's face.

There was also a man and a woman with them. She did not recognise the woman, but she knew the man. He was Simeon de Montford, a representative of Shivdler Legal, Kamran Dadashov's lawyers, the people who had taken her lovely Pimlico apartment from her.

She peeled away from the other mourners to meet them.

"Thank you for coming," she said.

Alexsei gestured to the woman. "This is Jasmine Kite, my legal representative. This is Mr de Montford of—"

"We've met," said Diana coolly.

Simeon de Montford gave a small thin smile of greeting.

"I thought we'd best get this done as soon as possible," said Alexsei.

The lawyer, Ms Kite, presented Diana with a multi-page legal document stapled in one corner. Diana was about to ask what it was but could clearly see the words 'tenancy agreement' at the top.

"I don't understand," she said.

"Alexsei's papa's people made a mistake," said Ariadne, coming up alongside Diana. "The agreement for the Ecclestone Square house should have been made with me, not you. All subsequent contracts have had to be redrafted. But with you as the tenant this time."

Diana frowned.

"The rent agreement for your flat," said Zaf. "Restarted, made anew. At the original, ridiculously low rate."

She couldn't quite believe it.

"I'm going back?"

"Unavoidably," said Simeon de Montford.

"I've known the pain of homelessness," said Zaf. "Believe me. Everyone should have the home that is rightfully theirs."

Diana felt a quiver of emotion run through her. Zaf reached out and hugged her tightly.

"It can't all come out right in the end like this, can it?" she said through the tears.

"With a little help from your friends," said Ariadne, joining the embrace.

Thank you for reading the London Cosy Mysteries series. Want to find out more about Zaf and his sister Connie, who's a detective constable in Birmingham? Learn all about the two of them and about the new series of books they feature in by joining my book club.

Happy reading!
Rachel McLean

Read the London Cosy Mysteries Series

Buy from book retailers or via the Rachel McLean website.

Also by Rachel McLean

The DI Zoe Finch Series – buy from book retailers or via the Rachel McLean website.

Deadly Wishes

Deadly Choices

Deadly Desires

Deadly Terror

Deadly Reprisal

Deadly Fallout

Deadly Christmas

The Dorset Crime Series – buy from book retailers or via the Rachel McLean website.

The Corfe Castle Murders

The Clifftop Murders

The Island Murders

The Monument Murders

The Millionaire Murders

The Fossil Beach Murders

The Blue Pool Murders

The Lighthouse Murders

The Ghost Village Murders

The Poole Harbour Murders

...and more to come

The McBride & Tanner Series – buy from book retailers or via the Rachel McLean website.

Blood and Money

Death and Poetry

Power and Treachery

Secrets and History

The Cumbria Crime Series by Rachel McLean and Joel Hames – buy from book retailers or via the Rachel McLean website.

The Harbour

The Mine

The Cairn

The Barn

The Lake

...and more to come

The Lyme Regis Women's Swimming Club Series by Rachel McLean and Millie Ravensworth – buy from book retailers or via the Rachel McLean website.

The Lyme Regis Women's Swimming Club

...and more to come

Also by Millie Ravensworth

The Cozy Craft Mysteries – Buy now in ebook and paperback

The Wonderland Murders

The Painted Lobster Murders

The Sequinned Cape Murders

The Swan Dress Murders

The Tie-Dyed Kaftan Murders

The Scarecrow Murders